To: Tashan

looking forward to
working with you.
You are a pleasure to
be around.

love
Alytia

The Will

Ornetta Simmonds

authorHOUSE®

AuthorHouse™
1663 Liberty Drive
Bloomington, IN 47403
www.authorhouse.com
Phone: 1-800-839-8640

First published by AuthorHouse   6/25/2010

ISBN: 978-1-4490-6214-9 (e)
ISBN: 978-1-4490-6205-7 (sc)

Library of Congress Control Number: 2009913391

Printed in the United States of America
Bloomington, Indiana

This book is printed on acid-free paper.

Book cover is a photo of early morning at Wingfield River in Old Road, St. Kitts.
All historical facts about St. Kitts are accurate. Reference to and about diet are also accurate.

For my Grandmother Isabel, my mother Shirley, and daughter Salonge.
You continue to inspire the people around you without knowing it.

Prologue

She was a mere 5 feet 2 inches and 125 pounds. The soft curls of her hair bounced on her shoulders and lightly caressed her face as she walked across the corridor. Her petite yet curvaceous body sashayed gently from side to side and left all those in her wake mesmerized. Everyone stopped what they were doing, and a hush came over the entire office. All that could be heard was the tapping of her heels against the immaculately tiled marble floor.

She had long passed the stage where the effect she had on people was shocking. She had learned to embrace her beauty and be humble about it. She smiled graciously and nodded at everyone she passed as the secretary led her to the conference room.

Her name was Atylk Summers, a name as unique as she was. As a child she searched to no avail for a meaning for her name, but as an adult she realized that was a good thing. It meant there were no limits or restrictions to what she could do. There was no one to tell her who she should be and so she embraced that knowledge and defined herself. Today she was a woman on a mission. She was a day shy of her fortieth birthday. You would never guess it, though; she looked like a thirty-year-old woman. However, when she spoke, it was with wisdom twenty years beyond what she should know. She had come a long way and had endured so much in life in preparation for this one moment. Today she would meet the Prime Minister of her country again, but under different circumstances. No longer was she the shy girl looking and longing for other people's approval. Today she had earned the right to chair this meeting. Today was the day her destiny would be fulfilled.

As she shook hands with him and took her place at the head of the conference table, she smiled at everyone and said a warm good morning. To her left was the Prime Minister, and to her right was the chairman of her organization, The Unit. Also around the table were all the people who had been working with her the past six months to make tomorrow's official opening a reality. Although they had been operating for the past four months, her PRO convinced her that this was the best way to generate media attention so that the public would be aware that such a place existed.

As her spokesman lit up the wall with the projector to show their plans and start the meeting, she interrupted for a brief moment to ensure the confidentiality agreements were signed and in order.

She had been busy for the past four months as well, grooming the children who would be there on the day of the opening. Quite a few of them had grown to love her and shared secrets with her that they had never told another soul. Keeping those secrets was a responsibility she didn't take lightly.

Although she was the brain behind everything, she was adamant this project not be about her, but rather the cause. As her spokesman proceeded by showing the 3D plans of the building, she had to blink quickly to rid a tear that threatened to spill over her eyelid. All the emotion she was holding in was making her weepy, and that wasn't good. She quickly cleared her throat and refocused her energy on the task ahead.

Chapter 1

"Wake up! Wake up! Or I'm going to leave without you. You have ten minutes to get ready."

She groaned, stretched, threw back the covers, and dragged herself out of bed. Atylk's mom was pissed this morning. Her legs felt heavy as they hit the cold floor. She was so tired. Her mom had kept telling her to go to bed the night before because they had to leave at 5:30 a.m., but there was so much excitement in her that she simply couldn't unwind enough to fall asleep.

The previous day she felt like the bravest little girl in the whole wide world. She had travelled to St. Maarten to meet her mom all by herself. Well, not really, she had air hostess assistance but nonetheless she was still proud of the fact that she knew exactly what to do to get there. After all, she had done it many times before. She quietly imitated the airhostess word for word as she gave the crew instruction. Not to mention the great view she had overlooking St. Kitts as the plane flew over one of its most spectacular historical sites.

The massive structure she had overlooked was both old with its ashy colored buildings and new with the lush green grass that was around it. From the vantage point she had in the air she could see clearly why it was such a compelling place to visit.

She had documented *Brimstone Hill's* long history in her note book but her notes didn't compare to the view she had of it now. Looking down she truly understood the meaning of the word 'fortress'.

Brimstone Hill Fortress was designed by British military engineers and built and maintained by African slaves. Cannon were first mounted on Brimstone Hill in 1690. The French had not considered it possible to transport cannon up the steep and thickly wooded sides of Brimstone Hill. The English construction of the fort carried on intermittently for just over 100 years. In its heyday, the fort was known as 'The Gibraltar of the West Indies', in reference to its imposing height and seeming invulnerability. In 1782, the French, under Admiral Comte Francois Joseph Paul de Grasse laid siege to the fort. During the siege, the adjacent island of Nevis surrendered, and guns from Fort Charles and other small forts there were brought to St. Kitts for use against Brimstone Hill. British Admiral Hood could not dislodge de Grasse, and after a month of siege, the heavily outnumbered and cut-off British garrison surrendered. However, a year later, the Treaty of Paris in 1783 restored St. Kitts and Brimstone Hill to British rule, along with the adjacent island of Nevis. Following these events, the British carried out a program to augment and strengthen the fortifications, and Brimstone Hill never again fell to an enemy force.

The fort was abandoned by the British in the mid 19th century, and the structures gradually decayed through vandalism and natural processes. Stabilization and restoration of the remaining structures started in the early 1900s. In 1973 HRH Prince Charles reopened the first area to be completely restored, the Prince of Wales Bastion.

Remembering her notes at a time like that would be upsetting to her friends if they knew what she was thinking, but she couldn't help it. She had a habit of zoning in and out of one thought or the other, which was something they often found quite odd and upsetting depending upon when she did it.

At that time Atylk didn't know that Queen Elizabeth II would unveil a plague naming Brimstone Hill Fortress a National Park or that it would become a UNESCO World Heritage Site and one of the best preserved historical fortifications in the Americas.

This was her fourth summer visiting her mom, who migrated from St. Kitts and left her with her grandmother at age five to relocate to the island of St. Maarten, trying to make a better life. She always felt so much closer to her grandmother than she did with Mom. Not because she loved one more than the other, but because she did so much more with her grandma than she did with her mom.

She was always excited to go take the goats on the pasture to graze whenever her grandma was taking them at mornings. Even more so, when they'd go to her vegetable garden after school to see how her crops were doing. There was just something about the way her Grandma said things that made her think about life in a whole new light. She never really said much, just phrases like "Any cry is cry as long as water runs." Later on in life Atylk realized her grandmother was explaining to her that she shouldn't laugh at anyone's pain, because real tears fall no matter who is shedding them. If she asked about Grandma's wrinkles she would shut her up by saying, "Pig did ask its mommy why her mouth so long and she said wait your turn."

As she grew and became an adult, she saw one mole too many on her face, and she realized that she was no longer a piglet. It was now her turn be the pig.

Oh my goodness, she thought. It was now 5:31. She had spent eleven minutes in the bath daydreaming. As she hurried to put her clothes on, she kept calling "Mommy," but her calls were greeted by an eerie silence that made her feel more and more uncomfortable. At 5:36, she ran though her mom's little house from room to room, becoming increasingly frantic as she got to the last room and realized her mom had left. Her mom never left her at home by herself. She was very protective of Atylk and knew the long hours she had to put in at work would be too much for her. Atylk quickly gave her laces a double knot and bolted for the door hoping she would see her mom walking down the street.

Her feet didn't seem to keep up with her mind. They needed to move much faster than they were moving now, as her mom was nowhere in sight. Later she would realize why this was so, but for now her fast walk had turned into a run. Her mom had been working as a nanny for the same family for the past four years, and the only time they left the house this early was when funds were low and they couldn't afford the bus. She was putting all the pieces together in her head as she ran. Should she ask someone walking in the opposite direction? She saw a lady in jeans and a red top walking towards her. No, she thought that would make others aware that she was by herself and they might follow her. Should she just turn around and go back home and lock the door and wait for her mom to come home? No, that wasn't a good idea either; she had already walked more than halfway to the job. Her heart felt like it wanted to burst out of her chest. The fear and sheer exhaustion from all that running was all too much for her. Her pace turned from a run to a fast walk to such a slow walk that other pedestrians began to pass her by.

There was a major intersection where all the traffic converged and with no traffic light she could only count on her mom for help to cross. Any other day the sun rising over the hills would looked beautiful, but today it seemed to hurt her eyes, and her cheeks felt wet. The sound of the car horns blaring so close to her seemed to echo in the distance. She heard someone on the nearby sidewalk asking, "Little girl, are you okay? Are you lost?" She swiped a tear away with the back of her hand in frustration. If only she had gone to bed early, as her mother had insisted, she wouldn't be in this mess. She turned around and looked up at the person talking to her. It was a sweet-looking middle-aged woman. But over her shoulder through the blur of her tears she saw someone else. She seemed to shrink in size, because her mother suddenly looked like a giant in her eyes. There she was: a concerned, almost frantic giant, with huge arms reaching towards her to scoop her up.

"What in the world were you thinking?" Her words were loud and raw with emotion, but her mother's voice never sounded so sweet in her ears. Her mom hadn't left her; *she* left the house in a panic, her mom explained. She simply went to the neighbor's house to ask her to collect a package when the mailman came around that day.

She promised her mom that she would never do anything like that ever again and that she would follow instructions and do as she was told. Atylk was all too happy to help her mom with her chores that day. Her mom was her latest superhero, who she was still idolizing because of this morning's rescue mission. She also knew that this coming weekend would be her weekend to shop for the things she needed to take back to St. Kitts with her.

Every summer Atylk and her cousin Madeline would leave their friends for just a few weeks to visit their moms. The visit was always exciting for Atylk, because she was not only going to catch up with friends she had come to know and love there, but their mothers would pack them up with new clothes, shoes, and school supplies to start the upcoming school year. Atylk was four years older than Madeline and so she always looked out for her cousin, like a big sister would. This summer Atylk would be making the trip twice. She was there now to get everything the family needed for her grandfather's funeral. But she would return later that summer with Madeline. Atylk's grandfather had passed away, and so she had to return to St. Kitts with her mom for the funeral. She never really knew him, though, because he had moved away to live in England long before she was born. She had never been to a funeral before, but she was pretty sure she wouldn't like it.

It was supposed to be a sad time. She understood that, but it also seemed to upset everyone in an angry way, including her grandmother. Aunts and uncles whom she had never seen before were at her grandmother's house, and there was constant arguing and bickering. Her grandmother said it was about the money her grandfather had left for her and it upset some of his children so much that they wanted to fight her. She offered to help her grandmother fight, but she simply laughed and said it wasn't that kind of fight. She tried to explain that it was a fight with paperwork, but it made no sense to her at all. It was all too much for Atylk, so she just went over to her friend's house whenever someone came over.

The following weekend when it was time to return to St. Kitts with her mother, they stopped at her friend Beatrice's house to say good-bye. Beatrice's mom always liked plants, and she arranged the ones in her home so nicely that they made the simple house seem so beautiful. From the walkway outside right up to the porch was lined with plants. She did it so lovely though. She started with small flower pots and progressed to larger ones until you were taken aback by the huge ones at the front door. She had matching flowers and pots on each side. There were more plants on the inside. One in particular stood out to her. It was a new addition and so she asked her friend when they got it. She said they had just gotten it yesterday and it was called a money tree. *Odd*, Atylk thought, she remembered asking her grandmother about that and she never really got the impression there was an actual plant called a money tree. Oh well. Atylk squeezed her friend tight, said good-bye, and then headed to the airport with her mom.

The following day, she attended her grandfather's funeral with her mother and the rest of the family. Atylk felt a bit guilty that she wasn't sad. Her grandfather had recently died after all, but she couldn't help it. Besides, it was hard for her to feel sadness, her grandfather was simply a face in a black and white photo, framed and hanging on her grandmother's living room wall. All she knew of him was what she heard in the adults' conversation. He had gained citizenship in England and became a wealthy business man there.

The morning after, Atylk went with her mom to the airport to see her off. On the way she yet again asked why the adults were sad one minute and then fussing and carrying on by the time they came home that same day. Again her mother's answers to her questions made little or no sense to her. She decided to change the subject.

"Mom, was Grandfather a good dad?" she asked timidly.

"Well, that depends on what you call a 'good dad.' He always provided food and clothes for us. Is that what you mean?"

"No, I mean did he play with you and tuck you in at night?" she pried.

"Well, not that I can remember, but that was hardly ever the case for any of my brothers or sisters, or for most of my friends now that I think about it."

"Well when I grow up and get married and have children I am going to insist that my children's father tuck his children in at night." Atylk folded her arms across her chest.

Her mom laughed and said, "Insist, now won't you? Where did you learn that word?" Atylk opened her backpack and flipped out the latest book she had been reading, beaming with pride as she held it up. "Mmmm, I see you're still into your books eh? Well good for you. You're still young, dear. When you get older you'll understand how things work in the adult world. Take me, for example; there is nothing I would love more than to be able to tuck you in at night, but I've got to work to ensure you have all the clothes and food you need, so we make do with the three months you come to see me for vacation. But let's just hope it's different for you, okay dear," she said softly, squeezing Atylk's cheeks between her palms while kissing her face. Atylk thought to ask about her own father, William.

"Sharon, your flight is being announced, you'd better go," her Uncle Marlo announced. They group hugged and Atylk looked and waved until she could no longer see her mother. Afterwards her uncle asked, "How is it that you never cry? Aren't you sad to see her go?"

"Yes, it hurts me here," Atylk said, touching her heart, "but I'm a tomboy, remember? And boys don't cry." Her uncle just laughed and ruffled her hair.

Chapter 2

Atylk's grandmother had always been a God-fearing woman, and so she insisted that everyone in her house attend church. It was such a part of Atylk's life that not going to church on Sunday would be as odd as seeing snow fall on her tiny Caribbean island.

With a population of about 40,000, St. Kitts was practically 85 degrees all year round, and what was so great about it, was that the island was only 69 square miles in size. You could always feel the fresh breezes from the ocean or the mountains caressing your face, and it felt heavenly. They had two seasons: a rainy season from April to September where they experienced a few scattered showers at best and an occasional hurricane at worse. The dry season encompassed the other months of the year.

St. Kitts was a country with quite a bit of history and was fast becoming a popular tourist site. Discovered by Christopher Columbus who then named it Isla de San Jorge in 1493 it was later colonized by Sir Thomas Warner. Warner was born in Suffolk, England in

1580 and travelled to the Caribbean in 1620 as captain under the command of Roger North. It was suggested that he try to colonize St. Kitts in 1623. Saint Kitts would prove to be the best-suited site for a British colony, because of its strategic central position ideal for expansion, friendly native population, fertile soil, abundant fresh water, and large salt deposits. Warner returned to England to gather more men to officially establish the colony. He was supported by Ralph Merrifield, a merchant, who provided the capital & Samuel Jefferson (the great-great-great grandfather of Thomas Jefferson, the 3rd President of U.S.A), who agreed to bring a second vessel with settlers and suppliers. He landed on St.Kitts on January 28, 1624 on the Hopewell and he established the colony then named Saint Christopher, the first British colony in the Caribbean. Today the island, once named Saint Christopher, carries the name St.Kitts.

In 1625, a French captain, Pierre Belain d'Esnambuc, arrived on the island. He had left France hoping to establish an island colony after hearing about the success of the British on Saint Kitts. Warner allowed him to settle on the island as well, thus making Saint Kitts the site of also the first French colony in the Caribbean. Warner also willingly accepted the French in an attempt to out-populate the local Kalinago, to whom he was growing suspicious of them.

The English and French joined forces and made a surprise night-time attack on the Kittitian Caribs. In the ensuing battle, three to four thousand Caribs allegedly took up arms against the Europeans. History reports that at a site now called Bloody Point, which housed the island's main Kalinago settlement, over 2,000 Kalinago men were massacred. The many dead bodies were dumped in a river, on the site which housed the Kalinago place of worship. For weeks, blood flowed down the river like water, giving it its nickname, *Bloody River.*

After the Kalingo Genocide of 1626 and the subsequent partitioning of the island Sir Thomas then shipped many thousands of Black African slaves. These slaves were then forced to work on the sugar and tobacco plantations. As the years passed Sir Thomas amassed a wealth in today's terms that would amount to over £100 million.

In 1643 Warner was made Parliamentary Governor of the Caribee Islands. He died on March 10, 1649 in St.Kitts and he was buried in a tomb in the village Middle Island. Today his tomb is one of the major historical sites on the island where tourists visit.

Although to Atylk this was all ancient history, presently there were still signs the islands historical richness all around her. Even the buildings that continued to be erected around the city were designed as a tribute to the country's rich heritage. Eighteenth century clocks and fountains were commonplace around the island. Exquisite architectural designs were in the columns and cornerstones of the building. A lot of thought especially went into highest floor of the buildings, just beneath the roof. Combining modern designs with legendry insignias was no easy feat. But the end results were unmistakably genius. So much so, that most people stood and looked up in awe of the artistry and architecture that went into the buildings.

However, summers were the most fun for her. This was the time when there was no rush to turn in class assignments, study for test or prepare for exams. She could stay far away from the hustle and busy streets of the city. There would be no cliché in 'smelling the roses', or in seeing the dew drops on lush green grass and exotic flowers that were all around the island. She could hear the continuous flow of the streams and the harmonious sounds of birds as they flew above her head. For this was the time when she could head to the mountains early in the morning with her friends to pick mangoes of every possible variety, stop on the way home and break stalks of sugarcane (her country's main export crop) simply for her eating pleasure, and be in the ocean by 10 a.m. The water temperature would be just right then. There was no need to pause for lunch; they had their lunch in their buckets before them. Enough fruit to last a week. Of course it never did, though. It was always a challenge to see who could finish theirs first. Today was one of those days.

This year Atylk would be turning twelve. All her friends, except for Shirley, still had a flat chest, with skinny legs, and did everything the guys did. Shirley came from a family where everyone was huge. Her father was 6' 5" tall, and all muscle. He worked security at a bank. Her mom stayed at home and took care of Shirley and her five siblings. At age twelve, Shirley was the oldest, and so she was expected to help her mom take care of the others after school and during the summer vacation.

Atylk could still remember that day when Shirley hurried them into the girls' bathroom to show them this thing that was "top secret." The girls all wanted to know what was up, still a little irked that this would take away from their recess time. Although they were all the same age, Judith was the smallest out of the four. Without even knowing it she was always somewhat bullied into things. No one really meant to; it was just that she was the lightest and smallest, making it easy to push her up a tree or slide her through the fence to unlock a neighbor's gate. Pam, on the other hand, was the "rich" kid. Not that she actually was, but in their minds it seemed that way simply because she was an only child and always got what she wanted. Atylk was the reader of the group, and because she read so much, she was the "go to" girl to ask questions about any and everything.

"Judith, check the stalls," commanded Shirley. Judith quickly looked under each door, her little frame bobbing up and down as she crouched down before each door. As she did the left side of the bathroom, Atylk kicked open those on the right, making sure no one was standing atop the toilet eavesdropping. They had done this so many times before. As she walked towards the last stall, the sound of a gasp made her turn around immediately. She rushed over to where Shirley was standing, blocking the door. It was the prettiest thing she had ever seen. Shirley had somehow managed to lower her tunic to her waist, and she had unbuttoned the top buttons of her uniform blouse to reveal a stunning white bra. They all knew what a brazier was. They had seen their moms' and grandmas' so many times while helping with laundry. But this, this was different. The only other person in their class who had breasts was Julie Marshalls, and she wore sports bras because she was fat. But this was the real deal. It was pinned up the back with hooks the same way the adults did theirs. And it was so white and lacy and beautiful. The "oohs" and "ahs" from the girls made Shirley beam with pride. Not only had never seen one this small—they never even knew they came in this size—but they were only ten years old. Although she was taller and bigger than the others, she wasn't really fat, like Julie Marshalls, and so none of the girls even realized she had started growing breasts or even needed a bra.

"My mom gave it to me last night. I could hardly wait to get to school and show you girls," she said excitedly.

"It's beautiful, Shirley," replied Atylk.

"Yeah Shirl, that's so cool," Judith joined in.

"Well, my mom says we're going to America next summer and I'm going to be able to pick up as many different colors as I want," boasted Pam.

"Shut up!" they all chorused.

They had gotten so used to Pam always trying to "one up" everybody that often times no one paid it much attention. But this wasn't the time for it. The sound of someone knocking on the bathroom door jolted them back to reality. Atylk asked them in an annoyed voice to hold on while Shirley quickly put her uniform back in place. By the time they headed to their lockers to get snacks, the bell rang to signal the end of break. The excitement of the bra exhibition was still in them, so no one really cared that much. No one except Pam, that is.

As Atylk sat on the sand with her cousin Madeline, who was eight, reminiscing about her grandfather's death and their elementary days, she was interrupted by the sound of screaming children. She turned to look. It was Shirley and her army. At least that's what the girls called her siblings. Shirley was now twelve; Fran was ten, Troy eight, Tricia six, and Nancy four. They had all thought that was it for her mom, Brenda, but then came little Zoe. She was only one. Shirley was so mad at her mom, because she was sure that after the two-year span had passed it was a signal that the "rabbit" was done. They would never dare call Brenda that to her face—they all loved her, and she was so caring and nurturing. It was just a joke between the girls. When Zoe came along the entire village adored her. She was the cutest baby ever.

"Where is Zoe?" asked Atylk.

"Sleeping," answered Shirley. "Mom will probably bring her for a dip later. Where is Judith?"

"She went to go get the boys and the tube," Pam joined in. "I'm going to ask my dad to get us our own tube. I hate when the boys start getting bossy about theirs."

"It's just a power trip for them," said Atylk.

"What the heck is a power trip?" asked Pam.

"You know, trying to be like the dads, telling us when we can use it, how long we can stay on it. All that crap. They just like the feeling of power it gives them to tell us what to do," Atylk explained.

"Well, my dad is going to get me one, then we'll see how much power they have," Pam chimed in.

"Yeah, yeah, we heard you the first time. Troy, didn't I tell you to keep an eye on you sisters?" Shirley screamed at her brother.

"That's a girl's job, and besides, Mom asked you to do it. I'm going to go catch some crab, for bait. When Damien comes down we're going fishing," Troy retorted as he proceeded to push rocks aside looking for crabs or worms for his fishing line.

Damien was in Troy's class and had twin two-year-old sisters. He was one of the four boys Judith went to go get. They all lived just a few houses away from each other. Trevor and David were bothers, fourteen and twelve respectively. David was the only boy of the group who was in the girl's class. Jason, their neighbor, was eleven. The girls often times teased Pam that maybe Jason is her brother because they behaved the same way. Although Jason had an older brother away at college he was the only child in his household and had that same self absorbed attitude that Pam did.

Atylk wondered what was taking Judith so long. From where they were sitting she could see the back of the houses in the neighborhood from between the coconut trees. But still no sign of Judith or the tube, and it was almost twelve o'clock. The boys promised to meet them there at eleven. They knew the girls were counting on them for a fun day, but it certainly wouldn't be fun without the tube.

"The tube" was the inner tube of a tractor's tire. The tractors were used on the island to transport sugar cane from the fields to the railway lines, where the cranes would then load the railway carts to be transported to the central sugar factory in the capital city, Basseterre. But sometimes a tractor tire would blow out, giving the kids of that community a chance to get the used tube from that tire. They would then put it in a big pan with water and wherever the bubbles appeared, that would be the place to patch. Once the holes were all patched, presto, a homemade float. It looked like a giant black donut, but for the children, it was the one thing they had to have to enjoy the summer.

Everyone knew how to swim by the time they were five. They learned simply by watching their friends and older children in the village swim. If for any reason you turned five and couldn't swim, you would learn by force. That's where the tube came in. It was strategically placed in the sea at a level where the children could stand. However, the innocent young children wouldn't know it, and as they thought everything was fine as they sat atop the tube, the older kids would tell them, "Listen, you need to get off, because we're going into the deep." As they realized the tube was heading further out to sea, they had to make a decision: swim ashore or risk being bumped off in the deep. Most times they were smart enough to swim as if their lives depended on it back to shore.

That was only one of the methods used to teach the children how to swim. Other times one was simply dragged out into the deep and dunked in the water. Therefore, they *had* to learn to swim away from those pranks if they didn't want to be dunked. Cruel maybe, but necessary. It was most embarrassing for a child, much less an adult, to live a hundred yards from the ocean and not be able to swim. So no one ever complained about the pranks, because the parents all understood that the tough love was necessary, and they also knew that they were a close-knit community and so no one would ever get hurt because they all looked out for each other.

A little after noon, Judith came running back to the sea holding her sister Lesley and her brother Tom with the boys and the tube in tow. It was time for the fun to begin.

They started the fun by playing a game of 'water dodge ball', giving the younger children a chance to enjoy *the tube*. The shrieks of delight and bellowing laughter couldn't be contained. The children splashed around in the water running away from the ball that was being tossed. Occasionally the ball would get tossed a little too far out at sea, and one of the older boys would swim to retrieve it. There was no stopping the fun however. That simply gave them the chance to sneak up on each other and hoist someone in the air, only to plunge them back down in the water. It was such a great accomplishment to be able to dunk someone. Not only did it take extreme strength, but it was most embarrassing for the victim, if he or she didn't see someone coming in for the attack. Or worse yet wasn't able to swim or squirm away from the prankster.

After playing for about two hours, and taking turns lounging on *the tube* when they got too tired, they got bored and were ready for a new challenge.

"Last one to 'the rock' is a rotten egg!" screamed Pam. She was so bad. They all laughed at her prank, because they were all guilty of doing it at one point or another. 'The rock' was a huge boulder that sat a quarter of a mile further out in the ocean from where they could all stand with the water touching their necks. No one knew for sure how it got there, but it was said to be a volcanic rock that landed in the ocean after an eruption. But for the children it was another way to be daring and fearless by swimming out to it. They could stand on it and the water would only swirl around their ankles. It gave them a chance to catch their breath, and then swim back to shore. Only Pam was already ten feet further out than they were, thus giving her a head start.

"Not fair, that's cheating!" Shirley yelled back at her. But as she was busy protesting such injustice everyone else dove head first into the depths of the clear blue water. Almost in unison, like a school of dolphins, the entire gang went chasing after Pam. Making white foam with each stroke of their arms. The boys closing in on her like sharks after a prey. Atylk was bringing up the rear and almost everyone was in front of her. Her competitive spirit refused to be denied that day. So arms and legs working in rhythmic togetherness, with her head swaying vigorously from side to side as she gasped for air, she soon gained ground on a few friends that were ahead of her. Her persistence paid off and soon she relished the laughter with the others as Shirley was the last to come in. The pain in her right leg however, made her think for a second that she might have overdone it a bit. She soon dismissed the thought as the new challenge presented itself.

"Last one left on *the rock* is a sour hog!" screamed Shirley at everyone. She knew she needed to redeem herself and didn't waste time idling. No one said it but everyone laughed at how quickly she changed from 'being fair', to at all cost, not losing the next challenge. She had gotten her head start this time around.

Atylk dove in the water again and within minutes she knew something was wrong. The intense pain coming from her right calf made her wonder for a second if a shark had sunken it's teeth into it. On impulse she pulled her legs inwards and reached for it with her left hand. Her calf was certainly intact, but she *did* feel something. She knew right away what had happened. She had seen this happen to her uncle Marlo many times before at home. Thing was, her grandmother was always there with a bottle of *something* to rub the pain away. She had pulled a muscle as her grandmother would say. Simply put; she had a cramp in her right leg. Today, however, she didn't have the luxury of medicines or her grandmother's comforting hand to massage it. Her problem was further compounded by the fact that she lost all concentration on swimming and was quickly sinking. She quickly collected her thoughts and realized that she was losing the opportunity to get help with every passing second as her friends headed to shore.

She squinted her eyes against the pain and tried paddling to stay afloat as she screamed for help. But to her dismay, no one looked back, or even heard her it seemed. They were almost at the sea shore. Sheer panic took her over and soon she was sinking beneath the water. Everything around her started to look dark. She opened her mouth to scream again but bubbles were all that came out as she sank lower and lower. The calm turquoise water was now a dark blue beast that was swallowing her little frame. As the salty water she swallowed scorched the back of her throat, she knew she was going to die.

Think, Atylk think. But no rational thought would come to her mind. What was once a sunny day suddenly looked quite dark and grim as she sank with certainty to her death. Then she remembered hearing her grandmother telling uncle Marlo to relax. As if saying it to Atylk now, she did. She relaxed. But as she did so, her foot touched the bottom of the ocean. She commanded her mind to think of a way out. Then she knew what she had to do. With her left knee, she bent it forward as far as she could. She was sure to let her right foot dangle, for she knew if she applied any tension to it the pain would get increasingly worse. She needed leverage to propel her body upward. As her bottom touched the heel of her left foot, with one fluid movement, she sent her body upward to the surface. They had played countless games where they challenged each other to see who could hold their breath the longest beneath the water. On a good day her best time was two minutes. But she was certain she had gone long past her existing personal record.

With her arms moving from her face to her sides in fluid circular motions she bounced to the surface like a ball someone was trying to hold beneath the water that had suddenly gotten away. She took in a huge gulp of air and automatically did what she needed to do to survive. She swung her body around and faced the horizon, then positioned her back, and legs above the surface of the water. She had to float her way to shore. It was the first lesson children had to master when learning how to swim. She used her arms like oars and little by little made her way back to shore.

As she faced the sky she could see now why everything was dark. The sun was replaced by dark clouds and she knew it was about to rain. Lucky for her by the time the first drop hit her face she had at least made it to a level where she could stand.

"Sour hog, sour hog!" her friends were chanting. She was too relieved to be perturbed by their taunts. However, Judith must have sensed something was wrong. She came over and asked,

"Are you ok? Don't look so glum, it's just a game."

"It's not that I got a cramp in my leg and I thought I was drowning," Atylk replied. The rain was beating down on their heads now. The younger children hated it and ran home, but the older kids simply dove beneath the water periodically to keep warm. Judith took Atylk's hand and led her out the water and helped her to lie down on the sand. Atylk touched the area where the muscle in her calf was bulging out and show her the direction in which she should massage it.

"Why didn't you call for help?" asked Judith.

"I did but no one heard me."

"Tell me when the pain goes away, because we have to head back in the water or we will freeze to death instead." Atylk knew she was trying her best to cheer her up by making light of the situation. But she still felt a bit shaky after the ordeal. Soon the pain subsided and they headed back in the water.

As suddenly as the rain had started it now stopped. The clouds parted to let the sun peek out again. Right before their eyes, the most intensely vibrant colors in a rainbow that they had ever seen, appeared. Some pointed to it, others just looked, spellbound!

Atylk's life's journey would have been so much easier if someone had told her then that this would be the underlining tone of her life's path. If someone had told her that there would be plenty of times that she would be alone, in trouble and would have to think fast and hard to find a way out, would she have believed them? Perhaps not.

As she looked at the rainbow, she tried to remember something her grandmother had told her about its significance and meaning. But she couldn't remember just then.

Chapter 3

As the summer progressed it was soon time for Atylk to go visit her mom and shop for all the things she would need to start school in September. This school year was special. It was the year the girls would all be going to high school. At that time there were only four high schools in the country, and so it was an honor and a privilege to be selected to take the big yellow bus to school.

This visit with her mom made Atylk feel just as special as Pam, if not more so. It was during this visit that it dawned on Atylk how much she really loved her mom, and how much her mom loved her. It was on this visit that her mom made sure she had everything she not only needed but wanted, and she hadn't a father like Pam did to share the expenses of sending a daughter off to high school.

Atylk's dad had migrated too. She wasn't sure when exactly but she knew it was before her mom did. She never remembered seeing her father before he went away. He migrated to the island of St. Thomas, which was too remote for her to visit. To get there she would have to get a visa, and he showed very little interest in trying to help her get one. She never really knew her father. He called her maybe once a year, and if he came back to St. Kitts to do business he looked her up. But she didn't know how to act around him. He was a stranger to her. There was nothing odd about that, however. It was a common thing to see mothers or just grandmothers raising children.

The first day of school was tomorrow, and although Atylk had everything new to wear, the physical pain she was feeling surpassed any possible excitement. Her head was throbbing and her stomach was tied in knots. She had always passed her subjects in school, and so she knew from science class that this day would come for all young girls. But no one told her about the cramps she would experience. As her grandmother came and placed a warm towel on her tummy, the pain subsided enough for her to sit up and sip some of the tea her grandmother brewed for her. It was the most awful tasting tea she had ever tasted, and she had tasted many of her grandmother's bush teas over the years. For the cold, there was a tea for that. If her skin stung, and she knew she hadn't been bitten, there was a tea for that. For vomit or diarrhea, there was a tea for that. So as bad as it tasted, she drank it because she knew that the pain would stop.

Sure enough, in an hour her grandmother was back to check on her, and although she wasn't feeling quite like herself, she felt so, so much better. As her grandmother sat on the bed next to her, the expression on her face made Atylk feel quite wary. Her grandmother was always full of life and bubbly, but this serious expression was new for her and Atylk didn't quite know what to make of it.

"Now listen here, this is the sign that you are becoming a woman. Soon you will be wearing the bras your mom bought you and start acting frisky to me. But mind you, I won't have any of dat nonsense under my roof." Her grandma paused for a minute, so Atylk butted in.

"What in the world are you talking about, Ma?"

"Hush and listen, child. I'm trying to tell you that your body is going to go through some changes and you're going to feel and act different. But the most important thing for you to know right now is that you can't play with boys. Yah hear me, child!" her grandmother shouted, after Atylk seemed not to be paying much attention.

"Okay, Ma," Atylk responded quickly. What her grandmother was trying to explain to her made no sense, but she was smart enough to know when to be quiet and listen.

The next morning, she drank some more of that awful tea, had her grandma's famous johnnycakes and saltfish for breakfast, got dressed, and headed outside to wait with her friend for the big yellow bus. She was about to cross the street when she remembered she didn't pack any johnnycakes for her friends. She quickly ran back in the house to pack some, only to find her grandmother had done it for her. A big smile spread across both their faces.

"Thanks, Ma. You're the best," she said with a sheepish grin.

"Can't see why you don't have a thing to worry about and yet you don't seem to remember where your head is from your elbow," her grandmother responded in her usual way. "Been spinning 'round the house all morning like a turkey without a head." To someone else's ears this might have sounded rough, but Atylk knew her grandma meant no harm.

Her friends would never forgive her if she didn't bring them any johnnycakes. Aunt Isa, as the entire village called her, made the best Johnnycakes ever. It was a simple mixture of flour, water, yeast, and salt, but somehow no one could make them the way she did. When asked what her secret ingredient was, she would whisper in your ear, "Love." That was just one of the reasons everyone loved her so. She always made you smile.

As the first day of school progressed, Atylk kept remembering that weird conversation with her grandmother last night. She was so distracted that her friends kept asking her if she was all right. As the bell rang for recess and she insisted the girls go on without her, the girls all came around her desk.

"Spill it," one of them said, almost hostile.

"I got my period yesterday and Ma says I can't play with boys," explained Atylk sheepishly. She knew it made no sense.

"What exactly did she say to you? I got mine a year ago and I still hang out with Jason and the others," said Shirley.

"I don't know, I don't know. I'm just telling you what she said," Atylk protested in frustration. She relived the conversation she had with her grandmother the night before, word for word.

"That's it?" asked Pam. She had had her period that summer too. Only Judith was left.

"For someone so smart you sure are dumb. She doesn't literally mean not to *play* with them; she's trying to tell you make sure you don't do the nasty with them," Shirley insisted. She playfully cuffed Atylk over the head for good measure. That put an end to all that awkwardness she was feeling, but often she couldn't help but wonder if perhaps her grandmother was the designated spokeswoman for Jesus, because she was always talking in parables.

True to the wisdom in her grandmother's words, the girls did go through those phases in bodily changes. Boys whom they had always seen as gross and disgusting suddenly gave them butterflies

26

in their stomach when they passed by. They were all suddenly careful about styling their hair. They always carried lotion and lip gloss in their back packs. But more dramatically, they started hearing rumors about the cool girls kissing boys and some even having sex. By the middle of their high school years, the girls just seemed to be doing so much more than Atylk. To keep up with all the discussions she read more books about such things. That way she seemed just as informed, experienced, and even more knowledgeable than the others.

The summer when she was about to turn thirteen, her dad had shipped her a package. In it were exercise books, a book entitled *Everything a Teenage Girl Should Know,* and pens—but not just any pen, *Cross* pens! They looked so elegant and expensive that she took one to school for the sole purpose of showing off. She never knew her father, but if only for that moment he was a hero in her eyes when her friends "oohed" and "aahed" at the sight of it.

The summer the girls were fifteen was one they would all remember. This was when they knew what their career choices would be, what their body type was going to be, and who they most wanted to date and possibly marry. Pam kept practicing her signature as Mrs. Winters, and it was no surprise that Jason Winters and Pam Douglas ended up a couple. They had gotten so much teasing about being so much alike when they were little. Shirley liked Trevor, but was unsure about how he felt about her since he was three years her senior. They would make a good couple when she got out of school, Atylk thought, because although Trevor was older, Shirley measured up to him in size quite nicely. Atylk professed her love for David to the girls, but she never told him. She just wanted to fit in and do and say what her girlfriends were saying. Truth be told, the only person who gave her butterflies in the stomach was Juan Walters.

But he was a city boy she had met in high school. Only Judith knew that though. It was considered wrong to date those city boys. Judith and Atylk had a special relationship. They kept each other's secrets. Judith was still a bit lanky, and so the boys didn't really show much love interest in her.

When Sam invited her to a party, Judith was beside herself with excitement. Sam was considered a popular kid and had quite a reputation with the girls in and out of school. Atylk thought it odd that he would ask Judith. Not that her friend wasn't beautiful, but the athletes and government ministers' daughters were more his type. She knew if she brought up that with Judith she would be accused of being jealous or something. It was no secret who this guy was, so she just figured she would keep her opinion to herself. By the time Judith told the other girls she had been invited to Sarah Bringham's party by none other than Sam, both Pam and Shirley wanted in. The problem was that this party was in the city. There was no way that their parents were going to let them go. Quite naturally, it was Pam who came up with the solution.

"How are you going to get there?" asked Atylk

"I don't know. I was thinking by bus, but then I don't know how we would get back." answered Judith.

"Hold up! There is no we, 'cause I'm not going," said Atylk.

"Why do you always have to be a party pooper?" asked Pam. "I know just how we can get there and back."

Atylk and the girls had grown apart somewhat, because Atylk was busy working at a scientific company in town so she could afford to pay for the subjects she had signed up for that upcoming June. Every subject in high school had to be paid for and passed in the final exam to earn one's diploma. It meant each student had to be much more accountable to succeed. Everyone else had gotten help to pay for theirs, but everyone else had both mom and dad around. Judith only had a mom, but her uncles were ready and willing to contribute. However, Atylk had only her mom, and it was too much money for her to pay alone, and graduating was too important to Atylk. She couldn't leave it up to chance. Her priorities had shifted. She didn't think or look at life the way they did. The work world made you grow up real fast when you realize money didn't just appear.

"It's not that—I love an adventure—but I've heard what goes on at these parties and I don't want to be a part of it!" she insisted. It was so dumb, she thought, that Sarah Bringham's dad was a lawyer, yet her parties were so lawless. I mean, they sneaked in so much liquor in her parties—and with her approval, no less. She often wondered if her dad really didn't know what was going on. If he did, would he cover things up for Sarah, or did he loved her so much in his own way that he *pretended* not to notice?

"Don't pay any attention to her. Tell me what you have in mind, Pam," Judith said.

"Well, Trevor has his license now, right? All we have to do is get Jason to borrow his dad's car," Pam suggested.

"Borrow or steal?" asked Shirley. "I don't want Trevor getting in trouble."

"He will never know. Jason says his dad can sleep through a hurricane," Pam said. "I don't know about you guys, but *I* want to go to this party. Judith and I are in, so let us know by the end of the week if you guys are going."

"What if we get in trouble? I'm going to get a beating from my dad," said Shirley.

"Come on, guys. This is a once-in-a-lifetime opportunity. Why can't you guys just be there for me? If we get a whipping, so what? At least it would be worth it," Judith said.

Worth it? Atylk wasn't sure about that, but she could hear the desperation in her friend's voice, and she certainly didn't want to be called a party pooper either. So by Saturday night they were all at Sarah's party. Atylk had to admit they had a fun time. That Monday, when they got to school, they all told their tale about how they *tried* to sneak back into their houses. Naturally they got caught. It was five in the morning when they finally got home after all. They all got punished, but Atylks punishment wasn't physical at all, yet she was hurting the most after it was all said and done.

You see her grandmother didn't let her in the house. She dozed on the porch right next to her grandmother's door, all the while begging to be let in. She knew her grandmother was up and could hear her calling. She always woke early.

When she finally opened the door at 6:30 a.m., all her grandmother said to her was, "Get in the bath and get dressed for church." She said nothing else to her that day, yet Atylk knew she had disappointed her grandmother terribly. Not only that, but one look at her grandmother's face that morning and she knew she hadn't slept a wink that night. Atylk felt so awful that she had put her grandmother through that simply because she didn't want to let her friends down. She learned a valuable lesson that day.

As December came that year, the strain of working and studying for her finals was getting to her. Atylk had budgeted carefully, so she knew that if she could work full time during the Christmas holidays, she would then be able to focus solely on her studies. She asked her manager for more hours, and he agreed. That way, from January onwards, she would be able to focus completely on her studies.

On Christmas Eve everyone would stay up late and redecorate their homes. Those who could afford Christmas trees put them up, but for the most part it was more about changing the draperies, laying down new carpet, and doing all the other little things that would prepare the house for visitors on Christmas Day. But as Atylk and Madeline worked with their grandmother to prepare the house, it was all Atylk could do to keep her eyes open. She was so tired from putting in all those extra hours at work that her eyelids felt heavy and ironing the new curtains was a task that seemed to take forever. When the final piece was hung, Atylk quickly went to her room and threw herself on her bed, clothes and all.

It was no surprise then that when Judith tapped and tapped her window later that night she failed to hear her. Judith's tapping had turned into a thunderous pounding, like someone trying to escape something. Was a dog after her? Atylk wondered. She groaned, turned, and snuggled under her blankets to get more comfortable. Surely she must be dreaming, but the longing in her friend's voice coupled with loud knocking on her window finally got her out of bed.

"Atylk, Atylk, for goodness sake open up. I need you," cried Judith, or at least it sounded like her. As Atylk opened the window the bright moonlight made the tears on her cheeks shine. Atylk just assumed it was from mere frustration at calling her for such a long time.

"I'm sorry, Judith, I was just so tired," Atylk replied weakly as she slid the window up and helped Judith climb in. As soon as her feet hit the ground in the bedroom, she threw herself in Atylk's arms.

Her body shook and convulsed and she sobbed helplessly. It was all so shocking to Atylk she didn't know what to do or say. So she just held her until her tears subsided.

"What's wrong, Ju?" Atylk asked quietly. Judith sat on the bed and wiped her tears with her hands.

"Remember I told you Uncle Roger … what am I saying? He's no uncle of mine! Well," she sniffled, trying her best to continue, "Like I told you, he's been drinking more and more lately." Judith hiccupped, still trying to calm herself down. "Well, he came home drunk tonight. I couldn't take it anymore, Atylk, he was saying the most awful things to Mommy." Her words were slurred and muffled by sobs, "So I told him not to talk to my mother like that. He turned on me and started saying, 'You think you're a woman now, is that's why you feel you can talk to me like that? Eh?'"

She threw her body on the bed and pulled her legs into her chest and hugged them. Her voice was deep and raw with emotion as she explained what happened next. "Then he grabbed my arm and told me this is what women get. He dragged me to Mom's room…"

Her tears started to flow again and Atylk just knew what she was going to say. Her body tensed in preparation for it. She never liked Roger. She knew Judith's other two uncles from the village, but Roger she had met only met a year ago, and he was the only one who lived with Judith.

"He raped me, Atylk." There was a long pause as Judith clenched her teeth, balled up both fist and hit the mattress repeatedly, shaking her head from side to side. "I hate him. I hate him! But you know what? I hate Mommy even more. I was reaching out to her, crying out her name, and she just turned and took Lesley and Tom to the living room. I kept calling her, Atylk. I screamed her name and she just turned the volume up on the television. I kept calling her, Atylk. Why didn't she come get me?" Her voice was so weak and helpless as she asked the question. Atylk wondered the same thing. Her heart ached for her friend.

As she helped her take a shower, she got the answer to why her mom didn't come and get her. As the shower beat down on her bruised body, Atylk couldn't see her tears, but she could hear it in her voice as she helped her wash her hair.

"You know what the worst part is? When he was done and I ran out to her she just took me to my room to *explain*"—she almost choked on the word as she said it—"to me that she just let us call him uncle, but he was actually her boyfriend. She didn't want her husband to know.

"'Things like this happen to girls sometimes,' she said. She was actually trying to justify it to me. Can you believe it? She said since Dad went to America he's been sending less and less money and we have to eat. I don't even want to see them. Can I sleep here?" Judith asked franticly.

"Of course you can." It was the least Atylk could do. She wished she could do more. Judith took the rag and scrubbed her body so hard that it made Atylk's heart ache. She couldn't believe that Judith's mom hadn't rescued her from that awful man. She couldn't have thought this was okay! She knew Judith and she knew that she felt dirty and that if she scrubbed hard enough she might feel clean again. Pam was the only one having sex. The other three girls were determined to save themselves for marriage. She could only imagine how awful Judith felt. It was so unfair. All Atylk could do after she got dressed was hug her as they both sat on the bed.

"I'm sorry, so so sorry, I'm sorry Ju … I'm sorry." The sincere softness in her tone coupled with the gentle way Atylk stroked her hair to dry it must have comforted her, because soon she was fast asleep.

To add insult to injury, two months later Judith found out she was pregnant. She never spoke to or looked at her mother the same after the incident, but worse still, her mom still allowed Roger to stay at the house. Although he never forced himself on her again, it was like a constant slap in the face from her mom every time Judith got home and he was still there. When her mom found out she was pregnant, Roger conveniently decided to migrate to another country to "help out" financially. Judith couldn't wait to finish school and move out. She made the tough choice to keep the baby, and Atylk did all she could to help her stay focused on her studies. It wasn't easy though. By March that year her tummy started showing and so she was teased and talked about constantly. The only other person in their class who had gotten pregnant and dropped out a year ago was Julie Marshalls. Everyone expected it somewhat because her body had matured so quickly, but Atylk was convinced it was low self-esteem that had caused it. She hadn't even gotten pregnant by one of their peers; it was by a grown man in the village. So many children didn't have their fathers around, and so Atylk always felt as though Julie was just looking for that father figure. She probably got caught up in something that was way over her head. It made Atylk so sad, because she had so much potential. She was always the one to sing their school song and national anthem. She had a beautiful voice, and Atylk and the other girls missed their classmate dearly.

Atylk was determined to be there for her friend. Whenever the other girls asked about it, Judith simply said she didn't want to talk about it. Eventually everyone got the message and left her alone. The school let her wear oversized clothes to minimize the teasing whenever she came into the city for school or any other purpose. That way only the people in her immediate village speculated why this happened or who had done this to her.

Their final exams came and went, and it was now time for them to go check their results. Atylk was by no means the smartest person in her class, but she worked hard and it always paid off. As she walked to the office to collect her certificate, she was shocked to see tears in the eyes of some of her classmates who she was certain would do well. What did that mean for her fate? she wondered.

As it turned out she did pass all her subjects and so with her graduation certificate in hand she was ready for the world of work. Hardly anyone could afford college, so it was imperative to pass one's subjects with greats high enough to get employment. For Atylk it was another mission accomplished.

Chapter 4

Atylk stood on the stairs in front of the Omni Insurance Company. If she landed this job it would be her first since graduating. She was a bit nervous about her interview, but she figured since she was early she would have time to calm down. However, by the time she got to the waiting area her palms were sweating. As she took a seat she saw a well-dressed young man, about thirty, leaving Mr. Bentley's office. Apparently she wasn't the only one being interviewed for this position. She had done a lot of research and knew she had the all the knowledge and the determination to get this job. She had been told the day before that Mr. Bentley would be the one interviewing her. The gentleman leaving the office seemed so put together with his laptop bag that suddenly she felt very unsure of herself. Her throat felt parched as the young lady next to her stood up and walked to the office. Atylk took one look at her long legs and cute business suit and instinctively crouched down a bit in her chair. Her skirt was a bit too short, in Atylk's opinion, but what if that was the look they wanted? She looked down at her plain gray suit and realized that her appearance paled in comparison. Her simple yellow button-up shirt was bright and brought a bit of sunshine to her look. Her skirt was knee length and hugged her curvy hips quite nicely. She tried to talk herself into calming down. What would he grandmother say to calm her at a time like this? She tried to remember one of her grandmother's parables, but none would come.

By the time the young lady came out of the office, she was smiling and cooing at Mr. Bentley. Atylk took a good look at her and noticed that she wasn't all that pretty, although her makeup was done perfectly. All Atylk had done to her face was apply some face powder and lipstick. As she stood up to enter, the light streaming through the window made the young lady's teardrop earrings glisten in the light, as if mocking her. Atylk touched her simple knob earrings self-consciously as she walked pass her. Then her grandmother's words come to her like a beacon of hope. *Stand tall child and don't you dare let nobody tell you who you are.* Atylk knew she was the right person for this job and she was determined to let them see that.

"Good morning, Mr. Bentley. My name is Atylk Summers. A pleasure to meet you." She was taken aback when she realized that the other members of the board were there too. She had done enough research and knew them all by name. She took her queue from their friendly smiles and went around the table, shaking their hands and addressing them all by name. They seemed pleasantly surprised and all stood to greet her before she took her seat.

"So, Ms. Summers, what makes you think you would be a good insurance saleswoman?" asked Mr. Bentley.

"Well, firstly, I think I'm a great people person. Second, I believe insurance could quite possibly be the best investment an individual or business could make, and more importantly, I believe Omni Insurance has the best deals available to any client," Atylk responded. Without looking directly at him, she noticed a hint of a smile on Mr. McDonald's face.

"So would you feel comfortable coming on board here? If so, why?" asked Mr. Bentley.

"Well, I'm a firm believer in helping others, and I know that Mr. McDonald has not only introduced life insurance policies for the elderly this year but has also been the major donor of scholarships among our high schools, and I think it speaks well of this company." As an afterthought she added, "Not that *I* was a lucky recipient of your generosity, but I forgive you for that." The all gave a little chuckle. "So that is something I would definitely want to be a part of."

"So have you given any thought to what type of insurance you would want to sell for us?" asked Mr. Krosby. He was the manager of the vehicle insurance department. "And if so, why would you want to sell that type?"

"Well, as a matter of fact, I think I would like to be under your wing, sir. Looking at your statements from last year's figures, I think you are not only quite a savvy business man, but I have quite a few ideas of my own that could take our profits to an even higher level. So not only would I be learning a lot, but I feel I could make a meaningful contribution to the company." Atylk squirmed a bit in her seat and wondered if she was going too far.

"Such as?" queried Mr. Krosby.

"Here's the thing. I'm looking at all the young people leaving school this year and they are so ready and eager to get out there and start driving—I think it's something we could capitalize on."

The three men looked at each other and shook their heads to say no. "Hold on, hold on, I know it sounds risky, but just hear me out for a minute. Obviously they would be high-risk drivers, but what we need to do is let them pay a higher premium, at the same time making it affordable by offering monthly as opposed to one-time payments."

"But how could that possibly be more profitable if we can't get our premium up front?" asked Mr. Bentley.

"Aaah, you asked the right question, Mr. Bentley. As my grandmother would say, 'Sometimes less is more.' I read in the news yesterday that Mr. Jenkins was opening a new car dealership to sell reconditioned vehicles. What we could do is enter an agreement with him to send his customers here to get insured. It's the perfect place for these young men and women to go to get their vehicle, because it would cost less, but they would still feel flashy in what looks like a new car. If we act before the other insurance companies we've got it in the bag."

"But there is no way for us to be sure that they will go there to get a car though," said Mr. Krosby.

"It's all about promotion, Mr. Krosby. If we put our advertisement out there that we are working in conjunction with Mr. Jenkins, it's a win-win situation for both of us. Mr. Jenkins gets free promotion and *we* get all his customers. Don't overlook the fact that *I* am one of those young people. So I *know* it's all about what the new trend is. As long as we get a few in, trust me, the rest will follow. These young people want what they want when they want it."

There was five seconds of silence, and then Atylk said in a cheerful but confident manner, "Oh by the way, did I mention that I want this job?" They all laughed, herself included.

"Well, I'm afraid you've left us no choice my dear. Welcome aboard." Mr. Bentley stood and shook her hand. It was all she could do to contain her excitement. By the time she left there she was walking on air.

They were so sold on her idea of monopolizing the insurance arena—by being the first choice for all the customers' insurance needs—that in no time she was promoted to second-in-command. She kept coming up with new and innovative ways to get new clients.

As her paycheck got higher, so did her fashion sense. She started dressing in such a sophisticated but eye catching manner that whenever she stepped out of the office, men would drive around the block just to get a second look at her. At first it seemed odd, but Atylk soon began to love the attention. She started to see herself as sexy and beautiful.

Today she was going to meet the staff that would be running the new branch opening in another part of the country. They had so many clients now that the branch in the city could not handle the burden. As she sat at the desk talking to Mr. Bentley, the sound of a deep raspy voice saying "good morning" interrupted her train of thought. She looked up to find standing before her, the most handsome man she had ever seen.

His name was Curtis Bradford. He was 5' 8" and all muscle. She was never the type to get nervous easily, but this guy made her nervous, and that wasn't good, not good at all. As it turned out his muscles were more intimidating than his personality, and they soon become close friends. They talked about everything, from politics to sports, and soon they were dating. She loved and respected him for the fact that he never pressured her to have sex. He would even let her sleep over if it got too late, and he was always the perfect gentleman. That's why Atylk knew she loved him.

Her love for him was soon put to the test when he got into financial trouble and without a second thought she offered to help in any way she could. She took out a loan to help him clear some excessive debt, which she wanted to pay back as quickly as possible she possibly could. So began her tiring life of working sixty-five hours a week, including a second job. She didn't mind, though, because Curtis was always fun to be around and he showed her a totally different lifestyle than what she was used to.

Curtis planned the most elaborate dates for her. He met lots of influential people through his work, and so he knew when and where the next big thing was happening. They dined on cruise ships that docked for the weekend. He took her to balls where she met ministers of government and even the prime minister himself. It all seemed so unreal to her—not the experience but the people. So many of them identified themselves solely by what they did or what their latest financial accomplishment was. Most came off as a bit shallow to her. She never told him that, though, because she knew he was trying to impress her.

Tonight they were going to the Governor's ball. Anyone who was anyone was going to be there. It was an honor to have your name written on this list, so as Curtis's name was announced he beamed with pride and showed off his lovely date, Atylk Summers.

He escorted her to the dance floor just as the musicians started playing a waltz. Atylk wasn't familiar with this style of dancing, so Curtis had generously paid for dance lessons to prepare them for this night. She danced gracefully, wanting to make him proud. By the time the dancing had ended and they had begun socializing, she was bored to death. She would have been three times as happy strolling in the park or walking across the beach barefooted—anything that would give her the opportunity to get to know Curtis better.

She listened to all the conversation going on around her and contributed only when asked a question. At times she wanted to erupt with a fit of laughter. At one point she had to walk away from a conversation between a couple of ladies for fear of embarrassing Curtis. One of the women was petite and the other was tall and lanky. They appeared to be in their mid-thirties.

"Latavia darling, it's been ages since I last saw you. Where on earth have you been?" asked the tall one.

"Oh, Niomi, bless my eyes, you're a sight to behold." They exchanged fake kisses on each cheek. Latavia continued, "The ambassador and I just came back from Hawaii. Marvelous vacation spot, dear. You simply must try."

"Ah, you're enjoying the delights of scooping up this country's most eligible bachelor, I see. Just how is that dashing husband of yours?"

"He's somewhere around here, mingling. Dare I say that purse is to die for. Where can I get my hands on such an item? Do tell." Latavia held her hands crisscrossed over her chest in a dramatic fashion.

"This one is a rare item, I'm afraid. One of a kind, handmade in Italy." Naomi opened it to show of the craftsmanship of its interior. Latavia placed both palms on her cheek and exhaled as if she was just given the most devastating news.

"But look at you, how did you get a shade of lipstick that matches your nails perfectly? That's such a beautiful shade of pink, with just a hint of beige. I love it," Naomi said, taking Latavia's hand from her cheek to examine her nails more closely. On and on they went. To think that society's best and brightest spoke in such a manner. She kept her opinions to herself of course. The last thing she wanted to do was upset Curtis.

Atylk was all too relieved when Curtis steered her away to introduce her to the governor and his wife. They were in a circle of people including Prime Minister St. Clair, Councilman Morris, and Justice Williams. As the introductions were made, Atylk was becoming exasperated.

"So, Mr. Bradford, you're an honorary invitee or—"

"No, no. We're with Omni Insurance, Platinum Donor for St. Christopher's Orphanage," Curtis answered. Atylk couldn't believe they had to justify their reason for being there.

"Oh yes, yes, Omni. You're the guys threatening to put Sloman's Insurance out of business," said the governor.

"It's called friendly competition, sir," Curtis said with a smile.

"Those guys have been in business for thirty-five years. It's no longer friendly when it threatens their livelihood," said Prime Minister St. Clair. "I hear this is your partner in crime," he said, tilting his head in Atylk's direction.

"Actually, I'm simply his partner at this time. No crime being committed here, just a woman hired to do a job—and who does it quite well," Atylk corrected.

"Touché, Ms. Summers," said Councilman Morris, tapping his wine glass to hers. She followed suit and soon everyone else was clinking glasses. She tried to hide the bored expression on her face all night, one of the longest she had experienced.

Chapter 5

It was her twenty-first birthday and Atylk was so excited. Curtis was planning a surprise party for her. She knew this, of course, because Judith knew about it and that automatically meant that Atylk knew. Judith quite naturally made her promise to look surprised when it all came together.

They had been dating for about two years now and in that time she found herself doing things she never thought she would. She felt like she had gotten so close to Curtis, who had become like her best friend. Her grandmother's health was ailing, and so between paying for her doctor's visits and medication, as well as her own personal bills, she was swamped. There was no other option if she wanted to help out Curtis but to get a loan. They were in this thing together and so his pain, his worries became hers. She understood why he might be in financial trouble and in some way felt responsible; after all, he was only trying to show her a good time. On their dates she simply saw him swipe his cards to pay for everything, but it wasn't long before she realized debt was a terrible burden to carry.

Often times she would take work from one job onto the other to complete on her break so that she would meet her deadlines. Sometimes she wondered if her assertiveness was a good thing. There was a new call center in town, and during training she was selected to be one of the supervisors. Although the pay was good there were so many responsibilities that went along with it that she wondered if she was biting off more than she could chew. She would rush from work at the insurance company at five and be ready for work at the call center from six to midnight. That left her with only five hours to sleep on a good day.

If Atylk didn't complain, Judith did. In fact, not a week passed by without the topic coming up about Curtis taking advantage of her. Atylk was only twenty-one and Curtis was thirty. Atylk didn't see anything wrong with the age difference, since they connected so much intellectually. Judith, however, wouldn't let up.

"Here's what I don't get: how is it that he makes no effort to come get you after a long, exhausting day?" Judith asked.

"I told you a thousand times, Ju. I told him I could handle it," Atylk insisted.

"I don't give a shit. Even if you told him that, a real man would make sure he was there for his woman!" Judith persisted. After she had her baby she was a changed woman. No longer did she take instructions from anyone, and she had gotten quite a foul mouth.

"Ju, could we please drop it," Atylk exclaimed, exasperated by the topic. "I love him and that's what people in love do. They're there for each other."

"I get the part about you *being there for him*, all right. I just don't see him being there *for you!*" Judith protested. "I just can't stand these brothers who can't man up but take advantage of younger women."

"Judith Angelica Martin!" Atylk was shouting now.

"I'm just saying. You can't beat a sister down for speaking her mind."

"Listen, I know you mean well, but I am okay with this. In a month I will finish paying off the loan for him, and I'll be back to myself again." Atylk unbuckled her seatbelt as they drove up to Curtis' mother's house. "Come on, let's go in. Remember, you have to lead the way so I can look *surprised*," she said, laughing.

She put on a surprised expression, trying to lighten the mood. As they entered the house, Atylk got into character.

"Are you sure this is where Mrs. Bradford wanted to meet us? It's so dark in here." Atylk said as part of her performance. As she flicked on the light quick they all shouted, "Happy Birthday!" True to form, Atylk jumped a little as if surprised. Everyone was clapping, but as she looked over to Judith, she saw her friend shaking her head as she clapped.

As the evening progressed, everyone got more and more intoxicated and so the spills began. Mrs. Bradford asked Atylk to grab some kitchen towels from the linen closet, and like an obedient daughter-in-law she hurried to get them. As she pushed the door open the sight of Curtis' shirtless torso was a bit startling to her, and for a minute she wondered if he too had an accident and came to grab a towel. When she heard the sound of a female voice, she instinctively flipped the closet light on. She was shocked, not only that Curtis would be making out with another woman at a place and time like this but more so at the person he was doing it with. It was Judith.

As he hurriedly put his shirt on, Atylk was furious. She could barely hear the words her friend was mumbling as she gave her the sign to get out. What she did notice, however, was the look on her face. She would analyze it and deal with her friend later, but for right now she had to deal with a more pressing matter.

"How dare you?" she growled under her breath as she approached him slowly.

"How dare I what? Feel like a man? We've been dating for two years now and every time I try to get close to you, you shut me down. A man has feelings, Atylk. Healthy feelings. The evidence of his arousal was apparent as he readjusted his pants and fixed himself, all the while glaring at her coldly. It was all she could do to keep herself from looking away in disgust. She wasn't going to let him off that easy.

"We talked about this, Curtis. You knew I wanted to save myself for marriage, so why didn't you say something then?"

"Because you're living in la-la land, and so I had to tell you what you wanted to hear!" he retorted. His demeanor was all so hostile and shocking that she wondered who this person was that was standing before her. However, she refused to back down.

"La-la land, is it? Since my world is so unreal in your eyes, Curtis, tell me this: was the money I gave you a few months ago fake too? Was the relief you felt to be out of debt a fake feeling for you? Heck, I can see now our whole relationship has been fake. But you know what, I know my feelings for you weren't. I'm so relieved to find out today that the only thing fake around here is you and that … that tramp out there!" She turned to walk away, then just as quickly swung back around and slapped him across the cheek. He didn't expect it, and the shocked expression on his face gave her a little gratification.

"Maybe *that* feels unreal to you too." With that she turned her back, walked out with her head held high, grabbed her purse, and left. They hadn't been exactly quiet in there, so as she was leaving some of her close friends gave her this pitying look. She just glared at them. She didn't know why she did it. Maybe she was angry at them too. She didn't give a shit. She was mad at the world right now, and all she knew was that she didn't want their pity.

Chapter 6

It had been a week since their break up, and for some reason not a single tear had fallen. She was hurting *so* badly inside, yet she couldn't understand why no tears would come. She had hoped that at the very least he would call and apologize, perhaps even call to see how she was doing. She kept looking at her phone expecting to see his number show up. But nothing. Not a word.

Oddly, the silence seemed to be a constant alarm bell blaring in her ear and there was nothing she could do to shut it off. She thought of all the long, tiring hours she put in at her part-time job. She thought of Judith badgering her about her being there for him. Finally, she looked at herself in the mirror and let out a loud scream.

It was a beautiful Sunday morning, and although she didn't feel much like going to church, she knew her grandmother and cousin Madeline were counting on her to pick them up. She had moved out from her grandmother's house after a year working at the Omni

Insurance Company. She had a twenty-year mortgage hanging over her head at a young age, but for Atylk it was an investment. She loved her grandmother dearly, but the house she grew up in was simply too small to accommodate her. She had to share a bedroom with Madeline, and as a grown woman she decided she wouldn't waste a dollar on rent but rather put that money into something she could later call her own.

Every Sunday after church she would spend the day with her grandmother and cousin if Madeline didn't have plans. This was her last year in school and everything was boring for Madeline (or as she pronounced it, "booring," always dragging out the O for effect).

Today Atylk really didn't feel like it, but she could just imagine her grandmother lecturing her. *The day you don't feel like going to church is the day you need to be in church. That's the day that you'll be blessed, and you know the devil ain't want you to get that blessing now. So get on over to that church, yah hear me.* At least that parable she understood, because for once her grandmother took time to explain it.

She only fully got it though when she heard the sermon that Sunday. Ironically, the topic was forgiveness. She hadn't spoken to Judith or Curtis since the incident. As the sermon went on she realized that everything the pastor was saying was true. Her refusal to forgive them *was* weighing her down. She was carrying the pain of it like a load on her back, so much so that by the time they got to her house, Grandmother took one look at her and said, "Whenever you're ready you going talk to me now child."

It was just her grandmother's way of talking, but somehow the word "child" was so annoying to her today. But more than that was the way her grandmother could read her expressions like a book. She always told her she wasn't meant to be "one of dem children for lying, 'cause her face told it all." She had wondered all that week if Curtis was right. Was she being naive and childish to believe she could wait for marriage to have sex? She talked it over with her grandmother, explaining what happened at her party and how she was now feeling.

"I always been proud of you, dear," her grandmother replied. "We ain't had much, but every day I sent you to school and like a sponge you took it all in. But with all the knowledge you got there, know this. The fear of the Lord is the beginning of all wisdom. There ain't nothing you will ever do in life that's more important than following the word of God. This too shall pass."

Here we go with the parables again, Atylk thought. Now that she was older, she thought it was the perfect time to ask her grandmother why she talked in this strange manner.

"Ma, I've always wondered, why is it that I could never get a simple answer from you sometimes?"

Her Grandmother reached into her purse for her Bible and flipped to a scripture that read, "He that hath ears let him hear, and he that hath eyes let him see." She interrupted the scripture lesson to ask for a glass of water. Atylk was anxious to get back to the topic at hand, and so she didn't realize she hadn't quite filled the glass.

"Pay attention. Go on and full this thing up," her grandmother said, holding the glass. As she finished pouring the water, her grandmother asked, "What was wrong with the glass you poured for me at first, Atylk?"

"Nothing. You just needed a bit more. Anyway, back to what I was asking you, Ma—"

"Back to it? We never left it, dear. It wasn't a full glass now, was it?" her grandmother asked.

"No, it wasn't," Atylk responded quickly, wanting to get back to the topic. Her grandmother banged her hand against the table.

"Wrong! It *was* a full glass. It was three quarters full." It startled Atylk a bit. Why was she getting so frustrated with her? There was an awkward silence as she proceeded to drink her water. After putting the glass back on the table, she asked, "Do you hear something?" She twisted her head slightly, pointing her ear toward a noise of some sort. Atylk couldn't hear a thing. They had only come in and sat down at the dining table. They hadn't turned on the radio or television. "Listen."

It was the last word her grandmother said before folding her arms against her chest and slouching back in her chair. A seemingly relaxing gesture, but her raised eyebrows said otherwise. So, she listened. She heard a dog barking and the sound of young children's carefree laughter outside as they played. She heard a car honk its horn as it passed by. Atylk was quite sure she said the world's longest 'ooohhh' out loud. As her grandmother turned the Bible around to her so she could read the scripture again, what the scripture was saying and what her grandmother's parables were all about. It was about thinking deeper thoughts, seeing things from a positive perspective, and listening to the sound of life and what it is saying to you. After that day she paid closer attention to her grandmother's parables, storing them someplace in the back of her head. Even if she couldn't decode them at the moment, she knew that they would come in handy some day. She even started recalling phrases spoken in the past and trying decipher them and apply them to her life.

The following weekend she invited Judith over for lunch. She had let go of the hurt and pain she felt from Curtis' betrayal, but she knew she needed to fix her relationship with Judith. "Blood is thicker than water," her grandmother would say. But she would also say, "Boyfriends come and go but friendships will last you a lifetime." She needed to fix this. It was only two weeks and already she missed talking to her best friend so, so much.

As the doorbell rang that Saturday evening, Atylk opened it and let her friend step not only into her home but into her arms and her life again. As the evening progressed, Judith explained what happened that night. She told Atylk that she just had a feeling Curtis was no good and wanted to prove it by seeing if he had the audacity to make out with her best friend. Atylk wanted to ask her so many questions. Like why she thought it necessary to use herself to prove he was no good. Or had that been the first time something like that had happened? But she didn't. Although the memory of the betrayal hurt, it was more important to Atylk to patch things up. Even so, Curtis was already rumored to be driving about in the car she helped him pay for no less—and with another woman. On their little island, everyone knew everyone, there were no secrets. He must have been seeing her all along if they were that close already. She was just glad he was out of her life and her friend was back in. She was ready to move on.

Chapter 7

Everyone's life seemed to take a different path as they got older. Judith was dating so many different people Atylk wondered sometimes how she could keep up. They were going to see Jeff, Judith's son, play football today. It meant a lot to him that his mom was coming to watch his big game. Judith never really spent as much time with him as Atylk thought she should. She claimed to be busy travelling for work, but Atylk thought differently. You see, Jeff looked nothing like Judith. He looked so much like his father that Atylk knew deep down that whenever Judith looked at him, deep down it was a reminder of her past that she wanted desperately to escape. So Jeff practically lived with his grandmother. Both Judith and Atylk hated his grandmother's parenting skills, but under the circumstances it was the best Judith could do.

Atylk hoped that one day Judith would be able to put the past behind her, because Jeff was nothing like his father. He had such a gentle soul. Always obedient and kind, sort of the way Judith was when she was a little girl. As he walked toward the court, Atylk thought she should give him a pep talk.

"Yo, Jeff, just remember, do your best. We can't ask for more than your best, and as long as you enjoy the game, that's your memory right there, all right." For added effect, Atylk balled up her fist and tapped her chest. He smiled.

"Don't listen to her and that psycho mumbo jumbo. That's just something people tell losers. You better get out there and whoop that other team. Yah hear me?" Judith said as she tilted her head to one side and raised her eyebrows at him. Jeff simply smiled even more and ran off.

"Now how you going tell that boy that?" Atylk asked her, smiling herself none the less.

As the game went on, both Atylk and Judith were growing increasingly anxious. The score was Visitors (Lions) 1, Home (Eagles) 0. Jeff's team was the home team, so winning today was a matter of pride. Both players and onlooker knew that. Jeff was doing a great job at defense—he always retrieved the ball—but no matter whom he kicked it, they couldn't score.

"No wonder they're losing," Judith exclaimed. "Do you see the size of those guys playing for the Lions?" She turned and looked at Atylk.

"It doesn't matter. It's a game of skill, not strength," she answered.

"Damn right it doesn't matter. What that dumbass coach needs to do is shift the game around and take Jeff off defense so he can score that damn ball!" Judith insisted. No matter how much Atylk told her to watch her language, it didn't matter. As if hearing her, with just fifteen minutes left in the game Jeff switched places another player and that's when things turned around for his team. As the announcer explained what was happening over the microphone, both Atylk and Judith were on the edge of their seats.

"And with just fifteen minutes left in the game, Coach Maddox gives the signal for a switch-player 12 with player 1, Jeff Martin. The whistle blows and there goes the ball. It's the Lions taking it to their goal. No, wait. Great steal by James Bartlette of the Eagles. Keep your eyes on him, ladies and gentlemen, player 5. Bartlette is not letting go of that ball. Can he do it? Yes! He's taking it the whole nine yards. He fakes player 7 of the Lions and gets the ball around him. What a pass! It's Jeff Martin, taking it to the Eagle's goal. Just ten minutes left, Lions coming in on the left and on the right. Martin pulls back the ball; he takes it to the left, no to the right. No one to block him now and he scores! WHAT A SHOT! Straight to the right top of the net. Looks like we're going into penalty, people. Let's wait and see."

Both Judith and Atylk jumped to their feet and high-fived each other.

"That's my son! That's my boy!" she said, beaming with such pride that Atylk couldn't help but give her a hug.

Meanwhile, Shirley was at home in her own warzone. Her two oldest girls were being prima donnas, as usual. As for the boys, well, that was another story.

"My hair is longer than yours," teased Abigail, stroking her hair playfully. She was Shirley's four-year-old daughter, although she seemed to think she was fourteen. Naturally, Sandra, who was five, had to put her in her place and show her who was boss. But that never really worked.

"No, it's not, that's why Mom always has to braid it," she replied in annoyance.

"It is too," replied Abigail, intending to win this fight.

"No it's not, and you know it so shut up!" said Sandra, who was growing increasingly upset.

"Don't tell me to shut up, big head." Abigail taunted.

"I just did. Shut up. Shut up. Shut up!" Sandra thought it was final.

"Shut don't up, prices do, so take your advice and do it too," Abigail sang.

"Mom!" Sandra cried out for help.

"Girls would you two knock it off," Shirley said, on her way to see what started *this* fight. Something her three-year-old boy was singing stopped her dead in her tracks.

"God made Adam, Adam made sin, God dug a hole and put Satan in…" Tony proudly sang to his brother.

"Where in the world did you learn that?" Shirley asked horrified. "You listen here, and you listen good. Don't you ever use the Lord's name in vain!" Shirley all but shouted down at their innocent faces. "Trevor, help me get these kids in the car before they rise my pressure up. You better talk to this boy. I won't have any of this nonsense in my house."

"I don't need to talk to him anymore. You've already put the fear of God in him. Look at him. He's about to cry." Trevor reached down to pick up Tony while holding Nathan by the hand to head outside.

"Well good. It's the beginning of all wisdom and he certainly isn't too young to learn that. Aunt Isa always says, 'You can't teach an old dog new tricks,'" Shirley said adamantly, try to sound like Atylk's grandmother. "They don't know right from wrong, so when they come home repeating what they see and hear it's our job to correct them. I'm sorry. I'm not going to wait until they are teenagers, when they think they know everything."

"I agree. Just go a little easier will you," Trevor suggested as he rounded up the kids.

At the same time Mrs. Pam Winters was in her penthouse apartment getting frustrated with Jason. Although she didn't want to admit it to her friends, they were desperately trying to have a baby and Jason wasn't following the schedule. He should have been home by now, since she was ovulating. She picked up the phone and dialed his number.

"Babes, I thought you would be home by—"

She was interrupted by his curt reply.

"I told you I would try. I have to wait for the night manager to get here. I can't just pick up and leave. If anything goes wrong I have to explain…" He couldn't go on because Pam quite naturally had to take control of the conversation.

"Well hurry home as soon as you can, okay?" The silence on the other end told her he had hung up. She hated it when they argued, but no matter how hard they tried things always seemed to go in that direction.

Chapter 8

This was the year the girls all turned thirty. Atylk invited them over for dinner that Friday night. Her birthday was the previous Wednesday, so she decided they would all have a cake each. Splurge a little. It had been years since they had had a sleepover and so much had happened. Naturally, Shirley did the cakes, making each cake as unique in taste and design as each girl was. Shirley's cake was a double fudge chocolate cake, with a bunny atop it and lots of Easter eggs all around it. Atylk's was an almond cheese cake with strawberry topping; the girls knew she loved cheese cake, and almonds were her favorite snack. For Judith a red velvet cake, iced with the word *'Palease'* in orange with a toy high heel shoe as the centerpiece; it was true to her bold personality and the diva within her. Pam had called Shirley two days before to ask for an upside down pineapple cake. That of course spoiled the surprise for everyone, but they were all still enjoying the evening. Enjoying it a little too much perhaps—they would all be putting in an extra day at the gym that week, not to mention the hangover they would surely have in the morning.

Pam had quite naturally married her high school sweetheart, Jason. They were always seen as the perfect couple. They moved to the city so Jason could be closer to work. He was the CEO of one of largest department stores in the city. Pam worked as the head secretary for one of the most prominent law firms in the country. They were so busy with their careers that they made no time to plan a family. They both had the highest position in their field, and they both loved their jobs and so everything else took second place. At least that's the story they told.

Shirley and Trevor dated off and on until they finally settled down when she had her first daughter. That was five years ago, and Shirley seemed to pop out a baby to mark each anniversary of their living together. Atylk's grandmother would say "The apple don't fall far from the tree." Of course, that simply meant that Shirley was just reliving what she had learned from her mom. Lesson being: a good woman knows how to make babies. The only difference was that Shirley didn't want to be a stay-at-home mom, so she worked as a supervisor at a bank. Atylk was so proud of her friend. Trevor was a fireman, but it was Shirley who brought home the most money, and it was Shirley who kept the house spotless, who baked all the delicious pasties for every party, and who had all her kids on time and on their best behavior for every and any occasion.

She was proud of all of them. Judith was the most famous face among them. She had used her slender figure to her advantage and became a model. Her face was on billboards, her photo in magazines, and she was sought out for all the runway shows that took place on their island. Her son Jeff was now twelve, but to look at her you would never believe she had a baby. She never spoke to Jeff about his father, although he had asked about him a few times. It was a topic she and Atylk debated about often. She knew he was a bit young to know the truth, but she didn't think it was a good idea to close the topic every time Jeff asked about it. She tried convincing her to at least explain that it was complicated, and she would explain when he got older. But Judith had become a very defiant person and she did what she wanted to do and said what she wanted to say whenever she felt like it. She understood why the topic was not up for discussion, but sometimes in life you have to face your demons. Atylk's grandmother would say, "You're only sweeping the dirt under the carpet." In other words, if you don't take out the mess, it's still there polluting the air—you just can't see it.

Of course Atylk had her own issues that she was dealing with, and she didn't wish to meddle in her friends' affairs. She just felt their pain and wanted to help wherever she could. But as she had learned from her grandmother, sometimes in life, no matter what you did or said to encourage a friend, they had to find the will within themselves to effect change.

Atylk had long since given up her virginity to her daughter's father. Her daughter Salo was now six. She had allowed her friends to convince her that since Kevin had proposed to her it was okay for her to lose her virginity. There were so many reasons they gave her. Firstly, the ring was a sign of his commitment. Secondly, she didn't want to marry someone who didn't have what it takes in the bedroom. The reasons went on and on.

She thought back to that morning after Salo was born six years ago.

"I don't know why I listened to you girls. Look where it got me—pregnant and alone," she had said. She tried laughing it off, but her friend detected the huskiness in her voice and so Judith added quickly,

"Palease! You're never alone. You've got us, right?" Just then her grandmother appeared.

"Do you mind, guys? I want to have a minute with Ma," Atylk pleaded.

"Of course," they all chorused. "Hi, Aunt Isa. We'll come back tomorrow, Atylk. Bye, Aunt Isa." One after another they said their good-byes to her grandmother, then left. There was an awkward silence.

"So how's you and the young one doing?" she asked.

"We're fine, Ma," she answered in a soft voice.

"You sure don't look fine, but if you say so, dear." Atylk didn't know if she meant her physical appearance or the turmoil and confusion on her face. Maybe it was a bit of both. She was in labor for almost eight hours, and through it all there was no sign of Kevin. He wasn't working that night; that much she knew. The rest was a mystery to her. Why didn't he pick up his phone when she called? Why didn't he respond to her text? She didn't want to assume the worst of him, but as Salo announced her arrival to this world with a loud cry, she was overjoyed yet saddened that he didn't care enough to witness it.

They chit chat for a bit before Atylk said what was bothering her.

"Ma, I've decided to call off the wedding." She didn't respond, so Atylk went on. They had been there for a while and still no sign of Kevin. Her grandmother never asked about him either. "I don't think

Kevin's capable of loving me the way I want to be loved. I just feel like I'm worth more than that," Atylk added.

Her grandmother let out a long sigh, then looked her dead in her eyes and sang her response in an all so matter of fact way,

"You're putting the cart before the horse, baby." Atylk hated when she chose these times to call her baby or child. It just made her feel even more vulnerable. "Only thing free in this world is salvation, and ain't nobody seems to want it. So if anyone offers anything for free child, you done know you better take two. And besides, I ain't hear nobody round here talking 'bout no wedding. I heard about a proposal, but no wedding. Ain't no use crying over spilled milk though."

Atylk had learned a long time ago to decode her grandmother's parables. This simply meant: She was finding out all this that she knows now, what she should have seen then, little child that she still is. She should have accepted the Lord into her heart as her savior a long time ago. Of course if she offers her body to a man he is going to take it and take too much of it. Kevin gave her a ring but never closed the deal. And lastly but by no means least: What's done is done and it's now time to move on.

She did feel like crying though. Instead she asked weakly, "Are you disappointed in me, Ma?"

"I ain't got no business judging nobody, child. I got my own sins. Ask the question again, but this time look up dear, just look up. Visiting time is almost over. I best be going. Take care of yourself now. You got to be twice as strong; you're responsible for two lives now." Her grandmother left, and almost on cue, in came Kevin. He was being all nice, and she responded in kind, answering all his questions. She never asked any though. She should have asked where he was last night when she was in labor. She could have asked why he didn't *bring her flowers. She would have asked why he was just now getting there, but then he said something that jolted her back to the present.*

"I've been secretly making our wedding plans, babes. I think you're gonna love it," he said with a hint of nervous excitement.

"There isn't going to be a wedding Kevin. I quit." Her two simple words must have hit a nerve with him, because he just stood there and kept asking her what she meant by that. He started apologizing for so many things that he had done wrong, some she didn't even remember. He apologized for the awful things he had said when he was upset. Those she did remember—like the time he told her she was getting fat and ugly while carrying his child. Or when he told her no one else would want her. Not that she believed him. She just didn't want to try looking. She loved him. She had risked putting her heart out there again, and again she was let down.

This time she thought it would work. This time she wasn't going to be childish in her beliefs. This time she would give him what he wanted and in turn she would get what she wanted—her happily ever after. After all, it was only fair. Her own father was absent from her life. If he couldn't love her, why should she expect that another man would? How would she even know what to expect if she had a man in her life? She was clueless. But she had a standard, and although she didn't know what to expect, she certainly knew what she wouldn't accept. This was one of them. She didn't care what her friends thought. She didn't care that this happened to women all the time. After leaving message after message, the silence of her cell phone was devastating.

He must have realized that she wasn't paying any attention, because she vaguely heard him saying "See you tomorrow" as he left. She wanted to burst into tears so badly. She looked down at Salo breastfeeding so peacefully in her arms. She reached out and touched her tiny fingers. Her little perfect ten tiny fingers. She bit down on her lip so hard she could taste the blood. She wanted to cry, she needed to cry, but no tears would come. She had never experienced pain like this. It was like someone was pounding her heart with a sledgehammer. How could she be hurting so, so much when no one was hitting her? She never ever wanted to feel this kind of pain again. Never! She closed her eyes tight for a quick second, unable to understand why no tears would come. But there was no mistaking the depth of pain she felt at that moment.

She was flooded with memories of how she came to be in this situation. After working with Omni Insurance for three years, Atylk decided she wanted to make a switch in her career — in part because it became uncomfortable working with Curtis, but there was also something else. She had decided to become a teacher. She couldn't explain it to anyone, but she felt she had no choice in the matter. It was like those people who went looking for volcanoes. Crazy thing to do, but the adventure, the excitement of finding and discovering new things beckoned to her. She just felt it in her bones that this was a path she had to take. It paid much less, of course, but true to her deepest inner feelings, by the end of her first year she realized she absolutely loved working with children.

There was something about the sparkle in their eyes and the excitement they exhibited after finally getting something she was trying to explain to them that was so intoxicating and invigorating to her. It just drew her in to love them in a way she simply couldn't explain to anyone. She watched them grow, innocently asking the silliest questions in their youth and then becoming shy and reserved as they got older, afraid of what their peers might think of them. It was at that juncture that she got the epiphany. She would start a boys and girls club. They so wanted to fit in, to be a part of something. It was a great opportunity for them to grow brave and bold and fearless, but by doing the right things. Staying away from gangs and instead forming study groups. Enjoying their gifts and talents for song and dance by performing for their peers, knowing all glory and honor belonged to God, who blessed them with such talents. That's how they inspired each other—by learning to win fights not with their fists but rather with pen and paper, in debates. These were the things that would help them in interviews upon leaving school, ultimately helping them to become meaningful contributors to their society.

Atylk had singlehandedly engineered the club to reach out to other teens. She printed T-shirts with their motto and logo: "Leaders, not followers." She consulted with them on their mission statement: "I can do all things through Christ, who strengthens me." They visited other schools, bringing their message to the youth. They had regular meetings, active debates and frequent trips and outings. Both she and the children enjoyed the joy of the Lord immensely.

Their first-year anniversary was coming up, so Atylk asked around trying to find a designer who was talented enough to complete the look they wanted in such a short time. In the end it was Judith of course who rescued her. She told her she knew this new and upcoming designer who had his own studio and workers. The part Judith didn't mention about Kevin was that he was French.

Atylk's virginity died the day she met Kevin Pierre. As Judith made introductions they shook hands, and the electricity between them was undeniable. By the time he spoke, even Judith noticed the way they were looking at each other.

"Please to meet you ma chère." He smiled knowingly at her as he looked into her eyes. She explained what she wanted for the students' outfits, all the while taking in his good looks and the talent and ease with which he was able to draw exactly what was in her

mind. He was handsome, but in a different way from Curtis. Curtis had magazine poster looks, but Kevin was good looking in a raw, masculine way. His hair was slightly curly and somewhat messy on top, as if he had run his fingers through it while in thought. His jaw line was nearly square, and his lips were thin and begged to be kissed. His tan complexion was a striking contrast to the dark hair of his mustache, and Atylk soon found herself looking down at the curly hair that peeked out from his shirt.

She didn't like where her thoughts were going, not one bit. As they headed back to the car, Judith smiled that coy smile and said,

"So....., you like Kevin, I see."

"Drop it," Atylk said firmly, then quickly changed the topic.

The rest of that month Atylk was busy finalizing plans for the club's anniversary week. She had found a sponsor to pay for the outfits and other expenses and kept a close check on how things were going with Kevin to ensure everything would be ready on time. She didn't actually go see him, concerned about the way her body reacted to him, and opted to call instead. He assured her that he would be ready.

The night they held the concert a few of her friends, who were also teachers at the school, were there to help and support the students. But five minutes before the concert began there was still no sign of Kevin. She was so utterly crushed and disappointed that she didn't know what to do. But the show had to go on. They were thirty minutes into the concert when Kevin showed up. Atylk should have asked him why he didn't answer his phone, but she was so relieved that he showed up it didn't matter at the moment. The play went off without a hitch to standing ovations and great reviews the following day. All in all it was a great week.

Kevin tried his best to get a date with her after that, and when he finally did, she realized that she was no match for his charm. In *their telephone conversations, Atylk shared her beliefs and principles about waiting to be married before sex. She was sure that would turn him off, but instead he said jokingly,*

"I guess you have to go out with me so I can see if you could be Mrs. Pierre, yes?" His approach was different from every other man she had gone out with. As charming as he was, he didn't pressure her in any way, not even for a kiss. For a second she entertained the thought that he was gay, but then quickly changed her mind one night when she gave him a hug. The evidence of his manhood was very apparent to her, and it became clear then that he liked her much, much more than he was letting on.

They had been dating for about three months now, and tonight Kevin was taking her to an intimate little jazz bar. He loved jazz, and on Valentine's Day, he thought it was the perfect place to take her. They had been dating for about a month and Atylk was already in love with him. She didn't physically show any sign of it, but deep down she thought he knew. Getting dressed for this particular night was a challenge. She didn't want to send the wrong message, but it was Valentine's night and love would be in the air. Wanting to look feminine, she decided on a pair of casual jeans studded with rhinestones along the sides from the waist to the hem. As an added touch, the back pockets had the same accessory. Judith would say her jeans screamed, "Bam! Check this out!" She settled on a white top that also hugged her curves nicely. She was sure everyone would be wearing red for lovers day, and that they weren't.

Always the charmer, Kevin told her how beautiful she looked as soon as he picked her up that night. Anyone else trying to charm her would go unnoticed, but Kevin had a triple threat that made her legs go weak. His French accent created this mystery about him that made Atylk want to discover his hidden secrets. All that night he spoke to her in a rich and husky tone that was all male. There was something about him tonight. He seemed like a man on a mission—a man with purpose. But then the last thing that took her down was the intensity in his eyes when he spoke to her. Yep, she was certainly in way over her head. But he was being such a gentleman that she felt totally safe, because she knew she would never make a move on him.

They entered the jazz club and sat at a reserved table. It had one of those curved chairs that allowed them to sit next to each other but also a high backrest that gave them privacy. He ordered them wine and a light dinner and talked about their day for a few minutes. As they ate the conversation turned serious.

"Atylk, it would be nice if we dated each other exclusively, yes?" he said in a tone that demanded she look at him.

"Well, I have been. Haven't you?" she asked, unsure where this was going.

"Yes, but that's not what I mean. I want to ... I need to know that the next guy that looks your way will see this," he pulled out a diamond ring from his breast pocket, "and know you are spoken for, yes."

Her features moved from a wide smile to a look of confusion to a tentative smile all over again.

"Wait a minute. This is all moving a little fast for me."

"Listen, I see the way the men look at you, and I know you need time to get to know me. I just want a commitment from you that we'll explore the possibility of us, yes?" There was something so endearing about the way he spoke that it made her stretch her hand out. He slipped the ring on her finger. It was a perfect fit. She had to talk to Judith. She excused herself and made her way to the ladies' room.

She quickly dialed her friend's number and all but screamed into the phone.

"He proposed, Ju—at least I think he did," she said.

"What do you mean? Hold on, let me get the girls on the other line," said Judith. Before Atylk knew it she was in a debate with Judith, Pam, and Shirley about what she should do.

"You have to head back out there. He's going to wonder what's taking you so long," instructed Pam.

"Wait, wait. Listen to me, just don't overreact. Enjoy the night and just play it cool," said Shirley.

"Don't tell her that. You know she is going to go back in there acting all stiff and guarded. 'Play it cool.' What the heck does that mean?" Judith was shouting by then.

"I just meant that she should relax for once and enjoy the moment," Shirley clarified.

"Well say that. Atylk, for once in your life, stop over-thinking things and enjoy the moment. Live a little. And by all means don't come home without a French kiss," Judith said, giggling. The others joined in on the laughter.

"Guys, guys, I gotta go. I don't know why I bothered calling you. You guys are making me more confused." She hung up, but she couldn't help smiling herself as she headed to their table.

The light music that was playing was silenced and the lighting changed, illuminating the crisp white shirt he was wearing beneath his blazer. Her white top glowed and made her look like an angel in his eyes, and for a moment no one else existed. A few musicians stood on the small stage and soon a gentleman came out and sat on a stool before them.

"It's Valentine's night, and I have composed a poem especially for the ladies tonight. It goes something like this..." The musicians began strumming their instruments and he began reciting from a paper in his hand.

"When?
When did I get to this place, where you're all I think about?
From the morning's light to the dusk of the night, and every hour between.
Your voice sets my heart a-racing, your smile sends the sun my way."

She looked at Kevin out of the corner of her eye and realized there was so much truth in the poem. It spoke to the emotions she felt inside. Kevin wasn't shy about it. He looked directly at her and then took her hand in his.

"When did my world become a place where the earth shifts beneath me every time you appear?
I wonder, is this a good thing? I've never experienced it before.
Should I hold on to you for balance, or should I run for cover because I'm scared?"

Atylk found herself snuggling closer to him. He smelt so good. Kevin simply slouched a bit more as if getting ready for what was about to come.

"When will it be okay for me to say what I feel inside?
How can I show you this thing I've tried so hard to hide?
What would happen if I did?
My heart, it's so precious to me. Why, I have no idea where this thing would lead!

Should I trust you, or would you make my heart bleed?"

He looked so handsome as the light danced across his face. The glow of the light on her blouse made everyone else disappear. He looked at her with such intensity that she couldn't look away. She dared not.

"When can I kiss you?
When will you touch me?
Oh please, don't make my heart ache!
I want this so badly
I need to feel your lips to quiet this quake."

The poet spoke the last line so softly and gently that it beckoned her to do just that. Tomorrow she would realize how corny this all was, but tonight with the music playing, the poet's way of reading—his voice rising and falling, quickly then slowly—the lighting, all put together with the wine, Kevin, it was like being under a spell. She couldn't help herself. She leaned in ever so slowly, and as her lips touched his, the magic began. The poet could have said the building was on fire for all she cared. She heard nothing else. It was just her and Kevin and the sweetest lips she had ever tasted. They were like honey in her mouth. She stopped for a second and asked quietly, "Can I do that again?"
Kevin simply replied in that husky tone, "You may."
Two simple words, and she was undone. All her reservations about this man and all her beliefs were breaking down, one by one. There was no turning back here. Something was happening to her, something strange yet wonderful. She squeezed her legs together and a moan escaped her lips. The sound of people clapping brought her back to reality. What the heck just happened to her?

"Could you take me home, please?" she asked anxiously.

"What's wrong? Did I do something wrong?" Kevin protested.

"No, it's not you; it's me." She stood up to leave.

"You didn't do anything wrong, ma chère," Kevin insisted.

"I know that," she replied. He didn't get it. Heck, she didn't get it. "Just take me home, please."

Something in her eyes must have told him something, because he just stood up, placed a wad of cash on the table, and they left.

By the time they got home and Kevin walked her to the door, Atylk was all set to say goodnight before she got in trouble. She turned around to face him and the look on his face was like that of a puppy who saw a bone and desperately needed it. She needed something too. She didn't quite know what it was, but she definitely needed something. He didn't make a move towards her, and it was this that intrigued her the most about this man. Kevin knew there was something unique about her too, and he was determined to find out, in his own way.

In no time they were in her bed. They did a frenzied dance to the music their bodies made. The music was loud and dramatic, but not loud enough to drown out the startled sound she made, turning pleasure to pain in an instant. Her body stiffened and Kevin stopped his dance too.

"Holy crap!" His fist gave the bed a big thump. He kissed her brow and kept telling her it was okay, saying it with such tenderness that she trusted him and soon relaxed. They finished the dance they had started, and by morning Atylk woke up with a wide smile on her face. It soon disappeared when she saw Kevin's face looking over her, seemingly upset.

"Morning. What's wrong?" she asked.

"What's wrong? Atylk, why didn't you tell me you were a virgin?" he asked.

"It doesn't matter. It's okay." She reached out to stroke his face and he sat up slowly and looked down at her.

"It's not okay! You are twenty-four years old, for heaven's sake."

"So?" she said, unable to understand why he was so upset after the beautiful night they shared.

He shook his head and said, "We'll talk about this another time. I've got to get to work." He stood up and walked to the bathroom. The sight of his body made a smile spread across her lips.

But they never talked about it. In fact, they did less and less talking when they were together. In Kevin's body, Atylk felt like she had just discovered a new kingdom she had to explore, and he let her. With all the patience he could muster he let her figure out new and more exciting things every time they did their dance. The pace changed sometimes. The way they danced changed at other times. The only thing that remained consistent was that she could expect something new, even though they had done it so many times. It was always exciting, and he always gave her the freedom she wanted to explore. That was the thing Atylk loved most about him. She knew she had broken her vow to wait for marriage, yet she lacked the will to stop herself.

Her phone awakened him one morning as he lay next to her. He picked it up to hear Judith singing "Happy Birthday" on the other end.

"How did you know?" he asked groggily.

"I'm supposed to know, you idiot. She's my best friend. Put her on the phone," Judith said in her usual brash way.

When Atylk was finished her conversation and hung up the phone, Kevin turned to her and asked, "Today is your birthday?"

Sometimes Atylk wondered why he got upset so easily sometimes. "Yeah, but it's no big deal. I never make a fuss about birthdays and Valentine's and stuff like that. It's all too commercialized. I think *any day should be a day to celebrate and buy something for someone you love. That way, if a day comes around and your pocket isn't right, there is no pressure because you've been showing love and appreciation all year."* As she rambled on, she didn't even realize Kevin was trying to show her his driver's license.

"You've got to be kidding me. Why didn't you tell me?" she said, amazed.

"I don't know. The topic never came up, and I don't make a big fuss about birthdays either," he explained, scratching his head. It explained so much. The chemistry between them, the way they always seemed to know what the other person would do or wanted.

Yep, Atylk loved this man with all her heart, and this, this was the proof that they belonged together. In his hand Kevin held his driver's license and the date of birth on it was the same as hers. All that differed was the year. He was six years older.

"Atylk, Atylk Summers. Could somebody palease tell me what planet this girl goes to sometimes?" Judith was asking the others. She was so deep in thought that she had forgotten they were still having their slumber party. They were all quiet, though, which was perhaps why she had drifted so far in her thoughts.

"Girls, do you think I'm fat?" Shirley asked.

"Of course not," Atylk said quickly. "You work out more than I do."

"I know, but I could never get down to your sizes." She circled the rim of her wine glass with her index finger.

"Don't beat yourself up. A lot of it is genetic. As long as you're healthy that's what matters," Atylk assured her friend.

"I guess you're right, but I can't help but wonder why, after four kids, Trevor won't propose?" she said softly.

"Get rid of him. I don't know why you keep him around. You've got a good job. It's not like you can't do without him," Judith suggested.

Sometimes Atylk felt as if Judith was on a personal crusade to hurt all men. After a brief silence she said, "Maybe that's the problem." Shirley looked perplexed. "I mean, maybe he *feels* like you don't need him."

"That's crazy. Trevor knows I love him," she dismissed the idea.

"I'm not saying he doesn't know that, but maybe he wants to feel needed. I don't even think you realize the way you talk sometimes. 'My house, my car.'" Atylk shrugged. She should be the last person to give advice. She knew Shirley meant no harm. She was just programmed that way. All her life she had been taking care of her siblings; it was just instinctively her nature to take control. But Atylk just felt that she needed to let up and let Trevor be the man in charge.

"It's not like he doesn't help out with the bills, and I count on him for so many other things with the kids. He's the first one to notice anything that needs to be fixed or done around our house," she insisted.

"You don't have to tell me. I know that. But have you ever asked him if he wanted to do something else? Maybe he has things he wants to do too. You know, dreams of his own. Listen, I don't know. I'm just babbling." Atylk decided not to go any further with the topic.

"Yes you are. Seems to me that I'm the only married woman in here," Pam said haughtily.

"Now why you gotta go there?" Judith said. Atylk knew she was ready for a fight.

"It's okay, Ju. She's right," Atylk said, wanting to drop the subject.

"No, she is not right. Why she always gotta try one up everybody? She's been doing it since we were kids."

Something about Judith's word must have gotten Pam thinking about her life, because she blurted out, "Jason and I have been trying to have a baby."

Everyone stopped what they were doing for a minute.

"I thought you guys didn't *want* kids," Shirley said.

"I just said that because we couldn't." She said it quickly, as if trying to get it out before she changed her mind about telling them. She then turned to Atylk and asked for her opinion. "What do you think we should do?"

"I thought you didn't care for her opinions," Judith goaded her.

"Well she's always reading something. It can't hurt to ask. Stay out of this," she snapped at Judith.

"Did she just tell me to—"

"Ju, this is serious. What did the doctor say?" Atylk asked.

"He said there is no physical reason why we couldn't, but we only saw a doctor recently," she informed. "We've been so busy blaming each other."

"I bet you were," Judith said.

"Ju," Atylk reprimanded, "Just keep trying. I'm sure it will happen eventually." She really wanted to tell her that she needed to relax and let it happen. Pam could be so uptight sometimes. But she could see the sadness in her eyes and decided now wasn't the right time.

"Could somebody tell me why this girl isn't married yet?" Shirley asked the others, addressing Atylk, while taking her hands and swinging them in a playful manner.

"Yeah, I could tell you." Judith came over to Atylk's side of the couch, hitting her with a pillow. "She's too deep. Prince charming has to ride up on his white horse—"

"What's wrong with that? His white horse could just be figurative for his car or something," Atylk insisted.

"Just make sure it's a Lexus or something," Pam put in. Everyone turned on her with pillows. She could be so vain sometimes.

For a few minutes they forgot their problems and were children again, playing and laughing. Atylk shared her own news by telling them that she was leaving and going to see her father. She would try to get her get her degree in the process and she had no idea when she'd be back. It was a good night, and they would all think back to it often.

Chapter 9

Atylk's big plan to find her father didn't turn out as she had planned. She had thought it out carefully and made the necessary plans to ensure she could support herself. All she needed was for him to vouch for her by signing a letter of recommendation. She had the money she needed to open a daycare centre, but with her just moving to St. Thomas she couldn't just open her business, because no one really knew her. That's where her dad came in. He was already established, and he simply needed to recommend her to the board of education.

She had spoken to him shortly after arriving on the island and they agreed she could come over for the Thanksgiving holidays. This was her father, the man who was responsible for bringing her into this world. She was certain that after spending time with her and Salo, he would realize what a mistake he had made by not being a part of her life—their lives. She knew she was lovable—her grandmother loved her, and her friends all loved her dearly too. Her father would love her too, because they were a part of each other. Their fates were intertwined.

She had spent the first three months making the necessary contacts to get her daycare up and running. She spent a substantial part of her savings on furniture, rent, and legal work. Her father's signature was all she needed to get her things going for her.

Salo and Atylk had so much fun that Thanksgiving weekend. There she met her mother-in-law, older brother, and two younger sisters. She even met a distant cousin. Other families came over to her dad's house with pies, cakes, main dishes, meats, poultry, and fish of all kinds in hand. They played racing games and board games of all kinds. Salo fit right in among the adults even on those board games. She helped her family's team win. As she rose to the occasion and answered her questions correctly, Atylk's heart swelled with pride. In the back of her mind she wondered if her father felt the same way about her. By the end of her visit she had had time to talk things over with her dad. He didn't actually say he would help, but he was supportive of her plans and didn't say he wouldn't help either.

The day came when she went to see her lawyer to finalize all the paperwork. He was in touch with her dad to make sure he received the documents and had in turn mailed them back. Her lawyer proceeded to open her dad's mail. She was so grateful to him and excited at the same time. As he unfolded the papers and flipped through them, a perplexed expression crept onto his face.

"What is it, what's wrong?" she asked anxiously.

"He didn't sign them." He seemed exasperated at the very idea. He was a professional and had never experienced anything like that. Not to mention the waste of time and money, money he knew she would never get back.

"That's crazy. Let me call him." She looked at her watch and knew based on the previous week's schedule that he should be home by now. His wife would be at work still, but her youngest sister and her dad should be there.

"Hello?" her sister answered.

"Hi, Abby. Is Daddy around?" Atylk asked.

"Hold on." Atylk could vaguely hear a short conversation in the background.

"No, he's not here," came the soft reply.

It came from a sweet gentle source, but it was the most brutal sound she had ever heard. She hung up, moved the phone from her ear to her purse, and instinctively put her hand back to her ear, hoping to stifle the ringing in there. This time the thought of tears never even crossed her mind. Her grandmother's spirit took over her every function. She stood up, straightened imaginary creases from her dress, shook his hand, and said thank you. She apologized for the inconvenience, and they explained pleasantries and she left the office.

She would never admit it, but her father not being there for her when she needed him most would be something she would carry with her for a long time. She was so hurt that she couldn't put it into words. How could she expect any man to love her unconditionally if the person responsible for her very existence couldn't care less if she died? No one asked her if she wanted to be here—she had no say in the matter—but she was born. She was there not for a hand out; she was a woman with ambition. All she asked him for was ten minutes of his time to read the documents, a pen and his signature. How could a man be so cold that when he sat at his table to eat, he didn't wonder if the child he had given birth to was okay? She didn't waste another minute of her time thinking about it, and pride wouldn't allow her to call him again for anything. It was time to press on.

She had enough money to last her another month, but after that she had no idea what she would do. She was in a foreign country, she had no friends and apparently no family. What would she do? What could she do? She looked at her options—all she had going for her was her health and strength. They were the only resources she had left and she was determined to use them. She was so frustrated, though, with the cards life dealt her. Salo would tease her at times that the world didn't like her at all, and although they laughed about it, she couldn't help but wonder if it was true.

Her perseverance paid off, albeit not in a big way. She took her glass quarter full and took a job she knew would never do back home. She became the cleaner at a daycare center. It didn't pay much, but it covered the bills for the time being. She was determined to survive, even if only by the sweat of her brow. In the two months she was there she received so many advances from men that she had to tone down her style a bit, just to blend in. Sometimes she felt so resentful towards men because of the way they approached her, as if she were a piece of meat. She had reached out to her distant cousin, whom she had met at her father's Thanksgiving dinner, and he was very willing and ready to help her. However, his conversations eventually became so sexually suggestive that she decided to cut off all communication with him.

She worked hard and she worked well. Her personality shined through, and soon she stopped cleaning and started working with the children at the daycare centre. After about six months, one mom in particular took a liking to her. Atylk just loved working with her two-year-old son, Danny. She recognized early on the he was extremely intelligent, even though his speech was delayed. The other teacher at the daycare didn't have the patience with him, and so Atylk took it upon herself to work as closely with him as she could. At age two he was already assembling puzzles made for five-year-olds. Although a bit shaky, you could see the numbers he wrote on his paper quite clearly. The extra attention Atylk gave him paid off, and by the time his third birthday came around he was speaking as clearly as the other children. You had to wait a little longer for his answers, but when he gave them the witty comments he would make brought a smile to her lips.

One morning after she got the children settled at their tables for their morning's activities, she felt someone pulling at her skirt tail.

"Tylk, David wants to take my paper. I want the red paper, Tylk. I don't want this green one." He shook his head from side to side as he spoke. She always smiled at the way he pronounced her name. He looked up at her and in the most endearing way said, "Could you please tell him he's not the boss of me?"

It was all she could do not to burst out in laughter. She walked over to his desk and reminded David that if he wanted a different color he should ask and not try to take Danny's paper. Danny sat back in his seat with a satisfied smile on his face and went straight to work.

His mom was expecting her second child and was thinking about working from home. She asked Atylk to become her nanny, and Atylk took the job. It did pay more money, of course, but more than that, she felt it was a privilege to work so closely with Danny. She couldn't explain why she felt this way, but she knew he was destined for greatness and it was an honor for her to be afforded this small role in his life.

After working with Danny and his sister Betty for about two years, Atylk realized she didn't play a small role at all. She got a firsthand understanding of why Danny's speech was so delayed. His mother had very little maternal skills and was so emotionally unavailable that Atylk's heart bled for the children she had now come to love. She had passed no judgment on the situation, but she did realize that although their dad did everything he could to make their mom happy, nothing seemed to work. The few times Atylk saw him smile or heard him laugh was while playing with his kids. They weren't exactly what Atylk would call rich, but they were definitely well off. Their house was well put together. If you were an outsider looking in, you would think they were the perfect little family. She was hired to take care of the kids, and that she did. She went over and beyond the call of duty, helping in every way she could. She did their parents' laundry when time permitted. She was constantly cleaning their bathroom, and she would help load the car with groceries when she was asked to work on holidays. She could take Salo to work with her on those days, so she didn't really mind that she was the only nanny working on days like the Fourth of July and so forth.

She soon noticed that their dad's personality was becoming more and more like their mom's. She hadn't taken a day off from work all year, but she had to have a minor operation and so she needed to take Thursday and Friday off from work. Atylk was shocked and hurt to realize that they had deducted money from her paycheck because of that. She called the children's father to find out why, and she soon wished she hadn't. His response was so cold that she wondered if this was the same man she had met two years ago.

"Well, certainly you wouldn't expect us to pay you and Nancy too," came the haughty, chilling voice on the other end of the phone.

Nancy was their weekend nanny who would be filling in for her. For their mom, it was a statement of her social status to say she could afford round-the-clock care, but for Atylk, it was all too sad to behold and be a part of. The children desperately needed that weekend time to interact with their parents. That was the beginning of the end for Atylk, and so when Christmas came around and she got no bonus, she just took it with a grunt. She did let them know when she came out to work that January that it was unfair and that they had treated her coldly. For her, it wasn't about convincing them to do the right thing but rather letting them know her mama didn't raise no fool.

She had prayed about it, because she was torn between wanting to quit and being there for the children. She had seen so many weekend nannies come and leave because of the poor attitude of the parents, and it took a toll on Danny emotionally. He couldn't understand why people just left. Naturally, she was the only person that noticed this, and it was so important to her to not walk away from him. As it turned out, they broke the news to Atylk that they would be moving in a few months. The children's mom had strategized this plan to hurt her by taking away her hours of work and giving it to the weekend nanny as some sort of payback for her daring to speak up for herself about the injustice she had faced. Atylk suspected she wanted her to quit so that she didn't have to pay her when she was leaving. For Atylk, it was actually a relief not to have to come in and see her all week. It also afforded her the opportunity to do work elsewhere, while not feeling like she abandoned the children. Atylk was determined not be another person to walk out of their lives.

The day arrived for them to move. They did something to Atylk that she was determined not to let slide. Upon taking the job, they both agreed that she would be reimbursed her travelling allowance.

But today, her paycheck had been shortchanged her transportation allowance, with the promise that she should come back later that day for it. They were short on cash, they said. She was sure to let them know what time she would be arriving, but when she got there and rang the bell she was told by the cleaning lady that they weren't in. Call it a gut feeling, but Atylk didn't buy it, and so she pretended to leave and waited a few minutes only to see the children's mother come down right on time to go pick up Danny from school.

Atylk smiled graciously at her as she approached her, only to be greeted by cold tone of voice. "Atylk, please, I can't talk to you right now, and besides if you think I'm going to give you any more money or any recommendation of any kind you've got to be crazy."

"Oh really now? I wasn't crazy a week ago when I was playing and laughing with and loving your kids. As a matter of fact, I think you are the only crazy person around here. Well, since I can't get a chance to talk to you here, I'll sit at Danny's school and wait for you. Maybe I can talk to you there." Atylk knew in her world, where impressions and people's perception of her was so important, this would be the last thing she would want.

"If you go to my son's school, I'm going to call the police." She turned and walked away.

"That's the best thing I've heard all day," Atylk responded. It wasn't that much money, but Atylk needed it nonetheless. Yes, sure she could let it go. But it was the principle of the thing that gnawed at Atylk's last nerve.

By the time Atylk arrived at the school, the children's mother was already there. Atylk was very good at reading people psychologically. She had learned this woman so well that when she looked through the school's clear window, she couldn't hear a word, but she could tell what was going on inside. She was holding her heart with both hands with a dazed expression on her face, and by the time she was through talking, the school's secretary took one look in Atylk's direction and picked up her phone. Atylk wasn't about to stoop to her level—she had too much class for that—so she waited calmly off the school premises for the cops to arrive. Two officers came and headed for the schools front door. Atylk waved to them, trying to get their attention.

"Yoo-hoo, over here. I think I'm the one you're looking for." She smiled her most charming smile. They didn't smile back but rather nodded their head in acknowledgement and went inside to get the story from Danny's mom—that her life was in danger no doubt. If Atylk wasn't so ticked off it would be almost laughable.

Shortly thereafter the cops came out to hear Atylk's side of the story. By the time she explained herself, she could see the look of empathy on their faces and they too agreed that an injustice had been done to her. However, they explained that it was a civil matter and their only advice was to take the matter to court. Atylk thought about it and realized that some battles weren't hers to fight. Some things were best left up to the Lord. So that day, she withdrew from the battle satisfied that she would live to win the war.

Atylk soon picked up a job at a restaurant. It was up and coming but new, and so the pay wasn't that much. But she was a team player and was happy to come on board and bring it to a higher level of excellence. She helped with everything. She cleaned, she cooked some of her grandmother's favorite recipes, and she helped with writing the daily menus and checks so they could get their supplies. She wasn't afraid to work from the bottom to the top. But almost a year later, a mere fifty dollars was added to her paycheck. She appreciated the increase, considering her starting paycheck was below minimum wage, but it certainly wasn't anything to rave about. She knew they were doing well, because their clientele had grown tremendously, so much so that her boss was building a massive house from the profits. She was certainly happy for him, but it was all the proof she needed that he could pay his staff better.

She was starting to get homesick. She didn't like this place anymore. She wasn't used to this dog-eat-dog place, where everyone used everyone else to propel themselves forward. She wasn't used to it and she didn't want to change who she was so that she could "make it." She was used to a place where you could go over to your neighbor's yard to get fruit or vegetables with a simple good morning and a short conversation to explain what you needed. It was never one-sided giving, either. The neighbor requesting vegetables brought fish if he was a fisherman himself or potatoes if he was a farmer. Their crime rate was close to zero. Very few people got divorced. Everything was just different where she was from.

It was one of those lazy Saturdays when the phone rang.

"Hello. Oh, hi Aunt Judith. You're here? That's great. Mom will be so excited," Salo answered. Calling Judith aunt was a gesture of respect they had all grown up with. Atylk scurried off the couch to get the phone.

"Oh my gosh. I can't believe you're actually here. When are you coming over?" Atylk was so excited to hear her best friend's voice on the other line.

"Yes, I came in this morning and I've got a few modeling assignments here in St. Thomas that may take me a month or two. But I want to take you someplace later. Can you come?"

"I think I can. The neighbor upstairs has always been kind enough to let her sleep over if need be. Besides, she loves playing with her girls." Atylk could hardly contain her excitement.

"Well great. From the sound of the e-mails you've been sending me, you need a break! I'll be by around 8. Same address right?" Judith enquired.

"Yes. I'll see you at eight." Atylk hadn't seen Judith in four years. She couldn't wait.

Soon after eight that night the bell rang and Salo peered through the door's peephole. She opened the door and threw herself in Judith's arms. By 8:30, Salo had brought out every possible award, certificate of achievement, and report card she had gotten to show Judith. Not only that, but she showed Judith her own personal Web page she designed for her school's upcoming computer science fair. With everything she showed her there came a story, of course, and Salo was so animated with her stories that it kept them both entertained. Atylk soon insisted she head upstairs for her sleepover. As she skipped out the door with her bag, closing the door with a loud thud, Judith turned to her.

"She has gotten so tall. I'm not at all surprised by her academic achievements, but my goodness, what a personality!" She smiled.

"Too much personality, if you ask me," Atylk responded.

"I wonder where she got that from," said Judith coyly.

"Hmm. I have no idea." They both burst out laughing. "As Ma would say, my dear, the apple don't fall far from the tree."

She shook her head with disapproval. "Palease, Atylk. I can't believe you're still quoting your grandmother. It was so uncool in high school, and it's certainly not cool now."

"You could say whatever you like, but look at what you guys and your advice got me. A baby and a life of struggle as a single parent. Ain't no advice my ma gave me that ever got me in trouble now." They both started laughing. It was hilarious how much Atylk sounded like her grandmother.

"Do you really blame us for what happened with Kevin?" asked Judith.

"Of course not. At the end of the day it was my decision to make, and besides, we were so young then that we didn't know any better. No one talked to us about love and sex. I was just so unprepared for the wave of emotion I felt. Although we thought we knew everything there was to know about life." She tried to impersonate her grandmother with her last statement. Judith just rolled her eyes telling her to quit it.

"How *is* Aunt Isa?" she asked

"Well, some days are good others bad. I just try my best to do what I can to help out financially. My aunt went back home to take care of her, so I think she's glad about that. There are days I miss her so much I can hardly bear it though," Atylk replied.

Their talk turned serious, and by the time Atylk unloaded what she had been through in the past years, she felt relieved and happy that her friend had stopped by. Judith also shared some of her traveling adventures with her, and they left Atylk with mixed feelings. After having her son, Judith, had become a bit promiscuous to say the least. She understood it, but she just didn't approve of it. She thought her friend deserved so much more. Atylk had a feeling that she was still using drugs. Atylk had bumped into some at her house while helping her clean up. Judith admitted that she did barely little occasionally, but she promised Atylk she would stop. It was such a big part of the lifestyle she lived that Atylk suspected she was just doing it to fit in.

In Judith's mind she was in control, doing just enough to numb her pain without having affecting her career. But hey, who was she to judge? Yet as she watched her friend, with her perfect makeup and designer shoes and bag, she had to admit there a twinge of envy formed within her. Not because of what she had, but because of how daring she was with men. She had fallen in and out of love too many times to count. Atylk doubted that she really was in love with any of these guys; it was all a big game to Judith. By the time their conversation was over that night, Atylk realized that Judith had a vendetta with men. Her "love them then leave them" approach was embedded so deeply within her that it seemed infectious. Judith was right—life was so unkind and unfair that there were only two options. You could either get hurt and be taken advantage of or you could strike first and get what you want at all cost and then make a quick exit.

"I have an excellent idea. I'm doing a gig at this club tonight. The boss is always looking for a new face to warm up the guys. Listen, you don't have to get close to them. You just have to work the pole and in a few hours you've made a grand plus in tips. I could so totally get you in. Besides, he owes me a favor," she said excitedly.

"I don't know, Ju. I'm not sure I'm right for this." Atylk thought about it for a second.

"What's there to think about? You said things were rough right? It's easy money. You are so beautiful the guys will throw crazy money at you. I'll be right there with you. I need to make some extra cash too. I've gotten so used to the modeling and fashion lifestyle that I had no idea how much debt I was in." She paused and stood up. "Palease, Atylk, give me a break. For once could you get off your holy horse and live a little?" She pulled Atylk off the couch. "We need to move now if were gonna make it. The warm-up show starts at 10 and it's now 9:30."

It was all happening so fast that by the time they got there, it was almost time for her to go on.

"Quick, put this on," Judith said. "Quick tips. For the guys, you just need to be their ultimate fantasy. Only you have the upper hand, because they can't have you. As far as the girls who work here, just stay out of their way and whatever you do don't piss them off. This is the top-paying club in the country and they've had to work their asses off to get here, so they know how to fight."

By the time she slipped into her red two-piece outfit, she realized she might as well be naked. It was too late to back out, though, because her name was being announced. Her stage name at least. It was all Judith's idea.

"Ladies and gentlemen, for the first time at Club Exotica, please welcome … *Lady Sensatious*." He said her stage name with such gusto that Atylk wondered if she could live up to their expectations. She took a last look in Judith's direction. She too was dressed for work and as she gave her the thumbs-up Atylk stepped on to the stage.

Her outfit must have been a hit, because the guys were in an uproar. Some even stood up. She had on a wig and high sparkly platform shoes to match her outfit. At first she was a bit shy, but the loud music, the whistling, and the money being thrown at her soon took her over, and she performed as though she had been doing this her whole life. In no time, it seemed, it was over. She got dressed, collected her money from the boss, along with what she made on stage, and was ready to head home. She went to the dressing room in search of her friend but didn't see her.

"Hey, Sensatious, you did good tonight," one of the girls said. "How about you stick around? There's a lot more where that came from. A few lap dances down here, or a few hours catering to their needs upstairs and you could really pull in some serious cash." Atylk had a feeling this girl was a veteran. She seemed to know the ins and outs of the business and she had the largest makeup station.

"No thanks. I gotta go pick up my daughter." Atylk turned to walk away when she saw her friend walking out of the shadows.

"That's not it. Why don't you tell them the truth. Why don't you tell them that you're too good to be here? Tell them what you really think about them, won't you?" Judith was taunting her of course, but this wasn't the time or place for it.

The woman speaking to Atylk suddenly stood up, very slowly. Atylk hadn't realized how tall she was. She towered over her mere five-foot, two-inch frame and she didn't like the feeling she was getting in the pit of her stomach.

"Is that right now? So exactly what is your opinion about us, *Sensatious?*" she sneered her stage name in a mocking tone. All the other ladies stopped what they were doing and turned to look at the showdown.

"Listen, I don't want any trou—" Her sentence was left incomplete as she turned around to the sound of a voice screaming.

"Police! Hands in the air, everyone on the floor!" Just then, the door on the other end of the long dressing room flew open and the security guy fired at the cop. She was directly in the line of fire. It was all happening so fast that Atylk couldn't comprehend what was going on, and she didn't drop to the floor in time. The sound of gunfire bellowed past her ear. As she dropped to the ground, she kept saying to herself, "This isn't happening. Oh God, I'm going to die. I'm dead now, I'm dead, I'm dead for sure."

The sound of Judith's voice screaming at her to shut up jolted her back to reality. She hadn't even realized she was speaking aloud. Atylk was certain that later, Judith would laugh at her reaction, but right now it was no laughing matter. The next thing she knew, the place was swarming with cops and they were off to the police station. As they were waiting to be booked and fingerprinted, Atylk took the opportunity to confront Judith about what had happened at the club. Judith was sitting directly across from her in the holding cell.

"I can't believe you did that to me. What's wrong with you?" Atylk said in a controlled scream.

"What's wrong with me, what's wrong with *me*? What's wrong with you? Why do you always have to play the victim, Miss Goody Two Shoes? Life has been good to you. You are drop-dead gorgeous, you have a beautiful, intelligent daughter, and yet you bitch about how life is unfair. If it is, it's because you want it that way. You have plenty of guys interested in you. Just marry one, for Pete's sake. When was the last time you got laid, Atylk? " Atylk turned her head away and didn't respond. "Thought so. Just one time, just one time you put your heart out there and you walk around like your vagina has been brutalized."

"It was twice actually, and please don't hate me because the choices I've made in life. I can't explain why my body is precious to me—it just is. I expect if I offer it to someone they will value it just as I do. Don't assume to know or even understand my pain. Besides, this isn't the time for this conversation. We're about to go to prison," Atylk said sadly.

"Hate you? I don't hate you. I wish I could trade places with you. You don't know what pain is, Atylk. Don't even give me that psycho mumbo jumbo about choices. Who gave a shit about my choices, huh? This?" She waved a hand in the air, gesturing to their surroundings. "This is a walk in the park. I've *been* in prison."

Atylk knew her friend had never served any jail time. She was talking about being raped and why her life was this way.

They were questioned separately, and although Atylk insisted she had no idea they were running a drug and prostitution ring, it made no difference. She was booked, photographed, fingerprinted, and locked away. She had no money for a good lawyer, so it was a month before the lawyer appointed to her was able to get her out.

Chapter 10

Day 1

That first night in prison, Atylk could hear her friend crying in the cell next to her, and so did she. It was a single tear that trickled down her cheek but a tear nonetheless. It was one of the longest nights she had ever experienced. She was given her one phone call and she placed a call to her cousin Madeline, giving her all the instructions she would need to come get Salo and take her home until she sorted out her life. It was a tough decision to migrate and take her daughter with her, but she knew there were times she wished she had her mom to talk to. Who knows? Maybe her life would have turned out differently. Not that her grandmother loved her any less, but at such a young age she just couldn't understand her grandmother's parables. She was certain to tell Madeline not to mention this prison thing to her daughter or her grandmother. It would break her heart.

Something else happened that night too. She felt the closest she had ever felt to the Lord. She talked to him and listened back, as scriptures she read as a child all came back to her. All the girls knew the scripture of John 3:16—they could recite it word for word—yet the magnitude of the sacrifice Jesus had made for them just passed over their heads. Any son or daughter would be honored to have their names written in their earthly father's will. Yet they didn't understand that their belief in Jesus's death and resurrection was their guarantee that they would have their names written in the Book of Life—in His will. The scriptures were there to teach her, to help her grow, not to harm her.

She had thought she had taken control of her life. Their big plan to strike first in the battle of the sexes had only backfired. There they were, planning to hurt a few nameless men's wallets, yet in the end they only hurt themselves. Look at the mess they were in now. It was so silly the way they envied each other's lives rather than appreciative their own.

She took heart in one idea: when you're at your lowest there is no place to go but up. She was ready for a change. She needed a miracle, and so as she lay awake that night she recognized that this was the right time for it. Sometimes in life we just need to be still, settle down, and calm down so God can perform that miracle. She noted the miracle of the fish and loaves, and how Jesus asked them to be seated first. She had some decisions and changes to make about her life—life-altering changes.

Day 2

The next day she spent most of her free time in the prison library. Her mind was overflowing with ideas, and she had to write them all down. There were plans she had to draw for a building and she was thankful that she had passed technical drawing in high school to help her complete this project, for it was quite complex.

By nighttime Atylk couldn't help but think of her daughter, Salo. They had been through a lot together. She thought of Salo's years growing up without a father. It was rough for Atylk, as she had to overcompensate for her father's absence. She bought her everything she needed and tried to be there for her as much as possible if she needed someone to talk to. By her high school years, however, it all threatened to backfire on Atylk. By encouraging her daughter to speak freely and openly, she gave Salo the impression that she could say whatever she thought to her mother.

It started when Salo was a child.

One day Atylk took her to work when she was only four. Salo, always fascinated with words, wanted to read everything. Everything meant everything! She sat next to her and read the sign on the bus that said, "No smoking, no eating, and no radios." And there began Salo's complexities about wanting to understand and dissect every spoken word.

"Mommy, can I use my Walkman? It plays music but it isn't a radio, is it, Mommy?" she asked. "Huh, Mommy?"

"Mmmmm," Atylk muttered. She was a bit distracted, so she just handed it to her.

"Mommy, are you eating, because the sign says no eating and you're chewing gum. Is chewing the same as eating, Mommy? Is it?" she asked, anxious for an answer.

"No, yes, I don't know. Could you just relax and be quiet for a minute, Salo?" Atylk needed some time to think about her day.

Salo looked at her watch carefully and a minute later said, "Mommy, could you tell that man over there to stop flipping his card. It's so annoying." She pouted. The man on the opposite side was in fact making a constant clicking noise with his bus pass.

"No, I can't tell him that—if anything, you're being annoying. Did I ever tell you that you talk too much?" Atylk was exhausted already and the day was yet young. Just as Salo was about to say something she got the glare and the finger over her lips—code for "not another word."

Her behavior progressed into her middle school years.

"Mommy, do you know what happened in school today?" she often asked.

"No, what?" Atylk would respond.

"I was selected to represent my school in a math fair because of a project I worked on with Jillian. But only one person can go, and because Ms. Jacobs selected me, Jillian was like, 'That's not fair,' and I was like, 'Well, I did all the work—you only brought the markers,' and she was like—"

"For heaven's sake, stop with the 'like.' You know how that annoys me," Atylk said.

Paying her no mind, Salo continued, "So after I couldn't take her whining any more, I was like, 'You know what, take it up with Ms. Jacobs, please.'"

"You know what? I really hate when I tell you not to do something and you still do it. There are so many words in the English language! Why do you young people have to kill 'like'? It's like people who swear. I always say it's because they don't know any other words to express themselves," Atylk went on.

"Well you just said it too," Salo retorted.

"Say what?"

"You just used the word 'like' in your sentence," Salo said. "And I didn't swear either."

"That's not the point!" Atylk persisted.

"Well it's your point. You said it." Salo would not give up. Atylk knew what was coming and she wasn't about to fall for it. Salo had to win every argument at all costs. Sometimes Atylk wondered if she would be a lawyer. She gave her the glare and pointed to her room. This meant, "Go think about it and come back."

By the time Salo's high school years came around, Atylk was frantic with worry about her child.

One day she came downstairs dressed in oversized everything.

"Good heavens, child, when I was your age I was so careful to look like a presentable young lady. What in the world are you wearing?"

"It's called clothes, Mother. I am so tired of hearing, 'When I was your age I didn't do this. When I was your age I didn't have that,'" she said in a mocking tone.

"Well, it's true I didn't even have a computer, and I think you ought to appreciate the sacrifices I made for you," Atylk pointed out.

"Well, I do. What do you want from me, a medal? I bring you good grades, don't I? You always say I need to bring you A's. I've topped that. I bring home A-pluses." Salo was raising her voice a bit now. She cocked her head to one side and asked, "Anything else?"

"As a matter of fact there is. First, lower your voice. Second, the grades you get are for *your* benefit, not mine. It makes me wonder how smart you really are if you can't recognize that. And third, grades come second to respecting your mother." She paused before adding, "I will always be here for you, Salo, but understand this. I am your mother, not your friend, and you are not permitted to say anything that comes into that little brain of yours to me. Am I making myself clear enough?" This time she was the one to raise her voice. Salo nodded her head.

"I can't hear you, young lady!"

"Yes, Mother," Salo agreed reluctantly.

"Now go to your room and put girl-clothes on your body," Atylk instructed. She was such a pretty little thing, but you'd never guess it, since she dressed more like a boy.

"Oh, and one more thing. I always tell you stories from my past and now may be the appropriate time to tell you this one." Salo let out a deep breath, as if saying, "Here we go again," but Atylk didn't care. She went on. "There was a girl in my school who was extremely intelligent and talented. She was called upon to represent the school countless times or sing the national anthem. But she was so smart that she outsmarted herself. She had a liking to this boy who didn't go to her school and she would always meet up with him at her friend's house. When her mom found out, she made her promise not to go to her friend's house. You know what she did?" she asked rhetorically. "She met up with him at *another* friend's house. She *thought* she was getting off on a technicality. But in the end, what she got was a baby, and she had to drop out of school."

"I guess this will all mean something to me someday, right?" Salo asked offhandedly. Atylk could have pushed the subject, but she decided to drop it for the time being.

Tonight, though, as Atylk looked around the four walls of her jail cell she thought she was her own disappointment.

Day 3

She sat next to Judith in the lunch room and the two women spoke about changing their lives and getting baptized when they got out. The church she grew up in didn't require that, but as she read the Bible for herself she realized it was a requirement. It was symbolic of her commitment to God, the way one might perform a marriage ceremony and pledge themselves to love and honor their mate. Only she would have no ring to prove that commitment. The proof would be in the lifestyle she lived. Judith agreed they needed to change course, however the bullies of the prison kept flicking pieces of their lunch in Atylk and Judith's direction. Some landed on their trays. Naturally, Judith wasn't having that. Talk of baptism would have to wait for her. Right now Judith had a fight to win.

Judith threw her tray straight at the face of the girl who was trying to pick a fight. It nicked her cheek but she simply used her index finger to swipe the blood and licked it. There was a sparkle in her eyes as she did it, as if it excited her somehow. Judith looked at Atylk and whispered, "You get the little one. I'll get Miss Vampire here."

"Get the little one. The only thing I wanna get is *outta here!*" Atylk screamed through her teeth. She wasn't afraid to defend herself, but they weren't in school anymore and she was just fed up with all the drama.

Judith dove head first, straight to her prison mate's midriff. Tables and chairs came crashing down, and a thunderous uproar of voices chorused, "Fight! Fight! Fight!" They kept their backs together in the fight and did their best to win, but they were outnumbered two to one. It didn't matter, though, because the fact that they stood up for themselves was all they needed to do to be respected among their prison mates.

Day 10

She soon began planning what she needed to do once she got out of prison. Many of these were practical concerns, but there were spiritual concerns as well. Her life needed balance. Naturally, she could strive to be happy, relax, find love, and increase her finances, but these things all came from external forces. But in the spirit, from within her, she would radiate joy, be at peace in spite of her circumstances, sow love on good soil (a God-fearing man) and expect a harvest, and whatever she touched would prosper.

All the sermons she had heard, combined with her grandmother's teaching, consumed her so much that she lay awake many nights. Sometimes she even skipped meals, because she just couldn't get away from the fresh revelations and epiphanies that came upon her. Her spiritual walk was no less important to the woman she would become.

Day 24

Her lawyer finally brought the news that she would be cleared of all the charges. It was a welcomed relief. She was so worried about her daughter and getting up and running again. Yes, she was a fighter all right, but this time around she wouldn't be fighting alone. This time around she would read her Bible and pray for guidance. This time around she wouldn't be doing what she wanted to do. Rather, she would follow His will.

Day 29

The last day before she got out there came a revelation that was so mind blowing that it made her smile from ear to ear. She knew that money didn't really make people happy, but it was necessary, and things sure were difficult when there was none. Just before she drifted off to sleep that night she remembered a conversation she had with her grandmother. With the sweet innocence of a child, she had asked her grandmother why was it that everyone couldn't have their own money tree. In her wisdom, her grandmother responded by telling her that just like Adam and Eve, man would find a way to kill it.

As she thought about that, it dawned on her. Everyone wanted to be rich, right? What if they were all given a million dollars at birth and told to spend it wisely. What if it was there in a trust fund and they didn't even know it? She calculated the average man's life expectancy (being three score and ten) and realized whether, directly or indirectly, even by virtue of going out and working at minimum wage, every man would earn his million in his lifetime. What were the requirements to achieve this then? Simple: a sound mind and body. *That* was the trust fund. God had given Atylk and her friends at the very least one talent: "a sound mind." They need only be thankful and use it to his glory. However, for the majority, that million would never come in one lump sum, because they bury that talent when they fail to invest and let their earnings multiply. When they fail to put their ideas into action they have killed their money tree.

It was such a deep revelation, and it gave her such peace and comfort, that she drifted off to into a sweet sound sleep.

Chapter 11

A math teacher once told Atylk that if she tried to solve a problem with a certain concept and got the wrong answer, it didn't matter if he changed the numbers in the equation. Her concept was wrong, and so therefore she would always get the same result, an x or a 0, because her concept of figuring it out was *wrong*. So after she got out of jail Atylk set out to think and approach life in a whole new way. She let the Christ in her shine through in everything she did.

She prayed about it and looked at the talents within her. She thought about what business she could invest in to enable her to fulfill her destiny. It had to be something that couldn't fail, something that would bring in money year round and wasn't just seasonal. She thought of man's basic needs and decided that if there was one thing a man needed to spend money on, it was food. Not another corner supermarket. There were enough of those. They lived in a time when no matter how sincere the intensions were, sometimes there just wouldn't be enough time in the day to prepare it. She had the answer: prepared food. She would open up her very own restaurant. Yes, there were enough of those too. However she would run hers in such a way that would set her apart from all the others. She had learned a lot from her grandmother's cooking and would be true to her favorite recipes: what made her food great was in fact her secret recipe, love. Her grandmother would preseason her meats the day before, or even a week before, to ensure it was perfect right down to the bone. At times she would stand at the stove for an hour if need be just adding her ingredients at the right time, stirring occasionally as it got to the right shade of brown. By the time she presented her plate it was a true labor of love.

She did her research and found out in a year she could save enough money to do this. Easy? No way. Possible? Yes! It meant sitting her daughter down and explaining the big plan and what they would have to do to achieve it. It meant doing simple things like making sandwiches at home so they would spend less when they were out. They bought everything wholesale, and Salo even volunteered to wear her school's uniform in an effort to save on clothes. It meant a lot to her that her daughter was on board with the plan and was even making suggestions. Sacrifice they did, but for Salo's sake, Atylk understood the importance of striking a balance.

There were four weeks of that year when the month had a fifth week, and so she would use that one paycheck to do whatever activity Salo wanted—a trip to the circus, a Broadway play in New York, it was her choice. The sacrifices they made those other weeks all seemed worth it that week when they were allowed to splurge. She used her department store cards just so she could get the discounts and specials, but she always paid cash. That way there was no interest at the end of the month. She even took in Judith as a roommate, but eventually she had to get someone else. Judith simply didn't look at responsibilities the same way she did, and she didn't want to ruin their relationship over something a trivial as money.

But through it all, she stayed focused on the task ahead. It was one thing to make these adjustments if you haven't tasted the finer things in life, but for her, it was a big undertaking to move from driving her car to take the bus or train, or eating at home when she was used to dining out. It would've been easier if she had had this revelation when she turned eighteen and was still living with her grandmother. At that time, she had no commitments, no bills, no rent, no child, nothing but a vision of what her life would be and a determination to get there.

After finding out that the average small business could be attained from one year of saving, she was determined to make it happen. She did not believe in going into debt. Her Bible told her, "It is better to lend than to borrow." The scriptures were her guide to success, making her decisions foolproof. Another scripture she held close to her heart was one that said, "The hand of the diligent maketh rich." Although she knew she would eventually earn that million in her lifetime, it would never come all at once if she continued to do what she was doing now. Plus, there was always that possibility that it wouldn't work. Then she would be paying twice for a well-intended venture if she got a loan. Had she done this at eighteen, that money would have doubled and tripled over and over by now. No, it certainly wasn't easy, but she was determined that a year of sacrifice was worth a lifetime of financial security.

For the first month she spoke to quite a few people who had small restaurants to find out what it took to make it happen. She took notes, and she went on the Internet and found out what everything she needed would cost. From the oven to the welcome mat, it was all recorded. She knew that if she shopped for most or all of her furniture and appliances in one place she would likely get a discount. She compared price quotes to see who would make her the best offer.

By the third month it was becoming all too much for her. Just saving wasn't enough. She applied her theory to little things. She did little things like run a snack stand on the weekends. That generated enough money to buy an ice cream cart by summer, and by the time that sixth month rolled around and she was making as much money on the weekend as she did during the week, she knew she was on to something. She was tired, yes, but more than that she was tired of just surviving. She was tired of giving her best and expecting the people around her to be kind, fair or even generous. She was tired of waiting for a better day to come. Since she would be tired anyway, she was intent on getting tired this time around by *making* a better day.

She had to make her restaurant different so it would stand out from the others. Accepting that what she wanted to do was an area in which she knew she was limited, she consulted with a nutritionist to put together a menu that was both delicious and healthy. They decided on a *Vegetarian/Diabetic Menu* and *2000 Calories Menu.* But Atylk was sure to include a *Weekend Menu,* which would reflect her heritage and give a bit of 'island flare'. Her homemade *Specialty Drinks* was an added bonus. They were a tropical delight.

It was important to her that her customers be informed consumers. So when designing her menu board she placed a tiny number above each recipe. On her menu flyers she placed corresponding facts that related to those numbers. On her Vegetarian/Diabetic Menu she explained not only how the dish was made but also included the corresponding fact that supported her decision to create the dish. Examples of such details included:

"In the past, many viewed vegetarianism as strange and faddish but appropriately planned vegetarian diets are now recognized by many, including the American Dietetic Association, as being nutritionally adequate, and providing healthful benefits in the prevention and treatment of chronic diseases.

A large body of scientific literature suggests that the consumption of a diet of whole grains, legumes, vegetables, nuts, and fruits, with the avoidance of meat and high-fat animal products, along with a regular exercise program is consistently associated with lower blood cholesterol levels, lower blood pressure, less obesity and consequently less heart disease, stroke, diabetes, cancer, and mortality. In African-Americans, the frequent consumption of nuts, fruits and green salads was associated with 35-44 percent lower risk of overall mortality."

For her 2000 Calories Menu, from breakfast to desert she also labeled the amount of calorie intake each dish included. Such examples included:

"Islander's Breakfast:
Omelet from three egg whites and one yolk with chopped onions, tomatoes and garlic, two slices of *Mama's home made* whole wheat bread with guava jam, natural fat-free yogurt topped with banana. Served with hot or iced green tea.
(570 calories)

Chicken Liamuiga Lunch:
Chicken pasta salad made with chicken breast, tomatoes, romaine lettuce, whole wheat pasta, and sauce. Served with mango, sour sop, passion fruit, or carrot juice.
(530 calories)

Chili con Carne Dinner:
Chili Con Carne made with red beans, onion, scallion, bell, chile, jalapeno pepper, ground beef, tomato sauce, and seasonings. Served with tossed salad and one small low-fat fruit trifle.
(800 calories)

Delightful Dessert:
Two slices of *Mama's* malt loaf (drizzle of butter is optional).
(200 calories)"

    This was just one of the many menus on a given day. For Atylk, she also realized the importance of establishing a website for the restaurant. Not only would it give more detailed information about the health benefits of her recipes but it would also help her promote sales. She intended to offer specials to customers who placed their order online. All her recipes were made 'to order'. Nothing was left for another day. If she intended to make deliveries it was critical that the orders came in with sufficient time in which to prepare them. That was the only way she would know how many pairs of hands she would need. Like everything else in life one can only plan to a certain extent, so it would be fourteen months before Atylk would be able to realize her dream of opening her restaurant. She knew something would always come up and she would have to spend the money she had planned on saving, so she was wise enough to eliminate the possibility of that happening by opening an account that placed a certain amount from her paycheck directly into a fixed deposit. There were times when food in the house was low, so she saved it for Salo and used the opportunity to fast and pray. There were times when she had no money for transportation to get to work, but didn't shed a tear; instead she stepped out on faith, singing songs of praise and reciting psalms and each time she was offered a ride to work. Salo would tease and say, "You sure make the devil mad, Mommy." But true to her commitment, the day did arrive when she could finally breathe a sigh of relief.

Her restaurant was small, but it was ideally placed in an area where all the major busses stopped. Sure enough word got around that her place was the place to eat. Seating was limited, and so most people just picked up their meals and headed home. It didn't matter, because before long they had their regulars and there was a line outside the door waiting to be served.

But it was her Weekend Menu that drew in the crowd. The weekend was Atylk's opportunity to pull out all the stops. That was when she would perfect her grandmother's homemade recipes. She made her grandmother's famous *Johnny cakes and salt fish. Her Cornballs with steamed fish and okras, Ackee and salt fish with boiled banana, Brown stewed red snapper with rice and beans, Conchs and dumplings, and the dish they couldn't get enough of was called Cook-up.* With every passing week the word spread about her restaurant, and Atylk was loving it.

The hottest day of the year came and they had their largest order ever to fill. They were catering for a wedding, and as if life was determined to prove it would give Atylk no breaks, the air conditioning broke down. Many prominent people would be there, so there was no room for failure. They had an hour to go before the food was scheduled to be picked up. It was like a furnace in the small kitchen. Atylk was taking a pot of water to the stove when some spilled over the top and she slipped and fell to her knees. The pot went clattering to the floor and water went everywhere. Her mind told her to get up, but her feet wouldn't obey. She felt a strange emotion come over her. Then suddenly it happened. She cried. She bawled, actually, and no matter what anyone said to her they couldn't get her to stop. Heck, she couldn't get herself to stop. Quite naturally her employees all thought something was seriously wrong, for they had never seen her like this before. But between sobs she assured them with a nod of her head that she fine. She signaled for them to go on working and they did. They all thought she was crying because she fell, but in fact she was crying because of the cards life had dealt her. She always gave 110 percent in everything she did—in her relationship, on her jobs—and instead of seeing the sincerity of her heart, everyone seemed to want to devour it, to take advantage of the kindness she offered.

She cried because she needed her mother sometimes and she wasn't there, and when all she wanted was a signature from her father, he wasn't there for her either. She cried because her childhood friend would rather seduce her boyfriend to prove a point than let her take the time she needed to get to know who he really was. She cried because when she was in labor with Salo, Kevin wasn't there. Not only was he not there, but she had to drive *herself* to the hospital. She cried because she wanted to give up. She was exhausted, physically, mentally, and emotionally. Tears were coming to her eyes in amounts that spilled over and drenched her shirt. She was all she had and the only person she could count on was herself. Right or wrong, the only way she could be hurt was to be foolish enough to let anyone get close enough to do that.

She needed a hug, though, and without realizing it her arms instinctively crossed over each other as she hugged her shoulders. Sadly it brought no comfort to her, because her hands were so rough that her palms and fingers pulled the fabric of her T-shirt. She looked down at her hands, and no longer did she see perfectly manicured nails. Rather, through the haziness of her tears, she saw chapped nails and her thumb had about a dozen little nicks on the inside where the knife she used to peel vegetables left its telltale marks. She thought she was all cried out, but the sight of her hands brought even more tears and sobs to the surface.

But someone was close, so close she could hear Him whispering for her to get up so loudly that she had to obey. How dare she throw in the towel? How selfish would she be to give up now when this was only a stepping stone towards the place where she was even more greatly needed? Salo certainly needed her for one thing. She remembered a love letter her daughter had written to her.

Dear Mom,

You always say you struggled with me. But I never felt it. I was the only one on my block when I was little to have a powered car. I always had birthday parties to celebrate each year. I even traveled. I just want you to know I love you and you are the best Mom ever.

Yes, often times the Lord uses the words and the innocence of a child to encourage you. It was that memory that got her standing. You see, when you're on your knees it's a good place to be. It's a place to do spiritual battles, a place to pray and regain your strength.

Atylk got so strong that day that by pressing forward she was able to open other branches to "Mama's Love" and soon there was a chain of her ever-growing franchise. One thing had to remain constant though—they had to cook with excellence. She was able to start off each employee by showing them what needed to be done to keep the integrity of the restaurant. Fortunately for her, everyone wanted to be rich, but no one wanted to put in the time it took to get there. So she did the work and was able to sell her restaurants for twice the amount it took her to start them. So it began that she had singlehandedly turned her life around with no one's help but God Almighty.

Her first sale was one she would always remember, and it set the tone for many business deals to come. Life had taught her enough to realize she now had to *assume* everyone was dishonest and then let them *prove* their innocence.

She had no money left to hire a good lawyer. She had pumped all her money into this new branch of "Mama's Love." She should really be moving into that new building herself because the first restaurant was small, but it had sentimental value to her so she decided to sell the new one and then do it all over again. She would be meeting with the first and only gentleman who showed an interest in buying the new restaurant. His name was Peter Harris. It was crucial that she made this sale. She had no money left to pay the workers that week. She knew they all had families that were counting on them. It was so nerve wracking that her hands actually shook as saw him walking in the doors of the new building. She whispered a prayer, stood up from the desk in the tiny office, and went to greet him. He was with his lawyer, and as the negotiation began she realized the price she quoted him would be taking her in the wrong direction. It was way lower than she ever thought.

"Listen, you gentlemen need to realize that the price I gave you doesn't even cover the qualified staff I will be starting you off with," she said, trying to sound calm and confident. "I would think you would appreciate that I'm starting you off on the right foot."

"Well, that's something we never really asked for now did we?" his lawyer was saying.

"I'm afraid that's simply a prerequisite to the deal on the table." She sat forward and leaned in towards them. "You see, as long as the restaurant carries this name, it's essential to its integrity to have a certain standard. Or else we might as well stop talking." The sweat forming at the tip of her hairline threatened to trickle down her forehead and reveal her nervous anxiety, betraying her calm tone.

Mr. Harris looked around trying to find something to complain about.

"Well, what about the cost to have this place cleaned up?" He pointed to the sawdust he could see through the glass off the office wall where the workmen had piled it up. "Not to mention I still have to buy pots and pans and so forth to get up and running."

"That is exactly why you were quoted the low price you got," she interjected. "Look, you have all the major appliances and a great staff that I can assure you will have this place in tip top shape for opening day."

So the negotiation went back and forth for an hour. Finally she got fed up and said, "Gentlemen, that's the price, take it or leave it."

His lawyer leaned over and whispered something in his ears. Then he said in a stern, chilling voice, "We'll leave it." She wanted to beg them to come back as she looked at their backs of their heads as they walked out, but her mouth wouldn't open.

She didn't sleep a wink that night. She kept going back and forth in her mind. Maybe she should call the lawyer and take the deal. After all, she had wages to pay in three days. She dismissed the thought, simply because she knew it was more than a fair price. She needed to make a healthy enough profit to do it all over again. She wasn't sure if she was doing the right thing, but she *was* sure about the potential for greatness within that restaurant. That was a fact she refused to back away from.

However, by morning she was at her wits end. She drummed her finger on her kitchen countertop as she looked down at the phone. She decided to dial the lawyer's number, then jumped as it rang just when she was about to grab it.

"Hello?" she inquired.

"Good morning, Ms. Summers. You sure do drive a hard bargain. My client has decided to take the offer. I will drop the paperwork over later this morning." He paused, then quickly added, "I'm sure you'll want to look them over thoroughly before signing, but we were hoping to have this wrapped up in time to open this weekend as the Music Festival will commence then. Good business sense, you know." She noticed he was rambling on, and then it dawned on her she had forgotten to breathe. She covered the mouthpiece of the phone with one hand and let in and let out three quick gulps of air.

"I'll be at my restaurant." They said their good-byes and while he slammed his fist on his desk and grinded his teeth in frustration, she hugged the phone to her chest and cried, "Thank you Lord," as tears ran down her cheek. They came so easily to the surface these days that it was as natural as breathing.

She later checked out Mr. Harris and realized he wasn't crying out for a lower price because he couldn't afford it. On the contrary, she found out he had made quite a fortune flipping houses and wanted to try his hand at something new. He had done so many business deals that he was certain that with his lawyer he could buy this restaurant for next to nothing. After all, they were partners, and that's what they did. Atylk left no room in her contract for him to sell this venture without her consent. They were both surprised that in her contract she took the time to explain exactly what was needed to run the business. It even came with a handbook that detailed how to train and groom staff, how to manage the finances of the business, and how to boost sales in tough economic times.

The investors didn't have to use her handbook, of course, but she had a lot of experience and she thought it could come in handy to help first timers at a venture of this nature. She didn't want to be selfish and not share what she had learned. In it were five major chapters:

1. Companies Are Only as Good as Their Staff

2. The Ideal Employee

3. Down to Business (Presentation, Preparation, and Profit)

4. Longevity (Cooking, Customers, and Capital)

5. Investment Ideas

It wasn't a long boring booklet but rather a direct approach to running the restaurant, detailing the small-business Dos and Don'ts that she was sure would leave any owner or manager inspired.

But there was something else she needed to do before getting to her ultimate goal in life. It was what she came to this island to get—with her father's help of course. Since she no longer needed his help, as far as Atylk was concerned it was still necessary to get it. It was a simple piece of paper but an important one nonetheless. She was going to graduate from college.

It was all just a formality, of course, because getting her associate's degree in business management would be child's play given her experience in business. Getting her bachelor's in business accounting would be even easier. What wouldn't be easy was getting her doctorate in child psychology. That she wouldn't do online. For that, she would enroll full time. It was too important to her.

Her friends were important to her too, but she was so busy that she couldn't keep in touch as she would have liked. Of course that was easier to tell herself than to admit she might need their help. Or even just someone to talk to. She certainly couldn't admit her dad hadn't lifted a finger to help her. She knew they would tell her she needed to start dating and make her life easier with someone's help. But she was determined to do this by herself. She was determined to succeed only by the sweat of her brow. And besides, she wasn't about to marry anyone for the wrong reasons. She would marry for love, and that wasn't about to happen either, for she had shut her heart off. That was the only way to protect it.

What she didn't realize was that way over in St. Kitts, her friends were having their own struggles. Just like her, they didn't want to bother anyone with their problems either. They weren't about to make themselves look bad in the eyes of their friends.

Chapter 12

Jason was sweating profusely. Today it was all or nothing. It was all the money he had left. Maybe the reason he wasn't winning was because he was betting too small. He just knew that by upping his game he would bring home some serious money. That would make his wife happy. Money made everyone happy, right?

As the horses galloped down the last stretch his heart pumped even faster, and a wide smile spread across his face. His horse was out front by a neck. His palms started to itch. This was the mother lode right here. All the months of bad luck was finally going to pay off.

Here she comes, you can do it baby, you're doing it girl. Yes, yes, you got it. Win this one for daddy.

"No, no, *noo!*" he screamed. Everyone was looking at him, but he didn't notice. His head felt light. Where the heck did that other horse come from? His horse was a sure win. He dropped back to his seat, defeated. He squeezed his ticket so tightly in his fist he could feel his nails digging into his palm. He was feeling so many emotions right now. Disappointment, loss, fear. How in the world was he going to explain this? He had to think and he had to think fast. But no thoughts would come; his mind was all blurry. He kept trying to think of something, something he could do to fix this. Something he could say.

Before he knew it, it was closing time and he was no closer to finding the answer to his problem. He had kept in touch with Pam's friends throughout the years and the only person he could think to call was Atylk. She wasn't much help though. He didn't go into details about the mess he was in, but she could hear the panic in his voice and simply told his to go home and talk it over with Pam. Pam would understand, she said. He wasn't so sure about that.

The only thing that could cheer him up a little bit was stopping in at his favorite restaurant before heading home. It wasn't his fault he had to eat out. It wasn't his fault there was never any home-cooked food at home. A man has to do what a man has to do. He had to eat, and eat he did. By the time he was finally ready to head home, he had polished off a chicken salad, then had the soup of the day—split pea soup. He had skipped his mid-afternoon snack, so he was just making up for it. He had a lousy waitress that night, though. She forgot his garlic bread. He had to ask her twice about it. He couldn't enjoy his soup without garlic bread. Then of course he simply had to have the chef's special—steak and potatoes. He *loved* steak and potatoes. He was a regular there, so he was always chosen to try out their new recipes. Tonight he got to try out their crab cakes. He took three of those. He knew he should be full by now, but strangely he wasn't. Dessert was next. His waitress gave him this incredulous look and asked him if he wanted it there or to go. Maybe he *was* eating too much. At his last doctor's visit we was warned that he was at the risk of a possible heart attack. His cholesterol and diabetes were at dangerous levels, but he couldn't think about that right now. He certainly couldn't take his dessert home; that would surely get him a lecture from Pam. He would simply have to deal with the funny stares he was getting in the restaurant. He tipped the scale at a whopping 395 lbs, but as he looked out the window and saw an obese gentleman passing by, he felt better. At least he wasn't that big—yet. Besides, he didn't look that awkward with his weight—he was tall and carried his weight well. With that rationale, he decided he was having his dessert right there.

* * *

Shirley was busy planning the weekend for her family. They were going to go to the beach and she had to make sure Trevor stocked up on everything they would need. She made the list and rushed into the den to give it to him.

"Honey, could you run to the store and pick up these things for me please? I'm going to go settle the kids."

"Sure, babes, as soon as the game is finished," replied Trevor, raising his hand to accept list without looking away from the television screen.

"But by the time the game is finished the store will be closed, and I need these stuff to prep for tomorrow," Shirley insisted.

"What's happening tomorrow?" he asked, still not looking away. "Goal!" he shouted, a wide grin on his face.

"We're going to the beach," she said. There was a loud thump upstairs, and she turned to look.

"Just when were you planning on telling me this?" This time he did look directly at her. There must have been something in his tone that told her to stop, because as she turned around she saw that he looked upset.

"But I always plan our weekends," she insisted.

"Exactly. Do you ever think to consult me on what I want to do?" he asked.

"This isn't about you. This is about the family. If you don't want to come with us you don't have to. It would just be easier for me if you did," she said, her shoulders slumped.

"That's not what I'm saying, babes. I'd never desert you and the kids. I would just like a chance to plan what we're going to do for a change, or at the very least you can ask me if I'm all right with your plans." He turned the television off and stormed past her towards the door.

"Honey, can we talk about this?" She knew he was angry, and it was the last thing she needed right now. The slam of the front door was the only answer she got.

* * *

Judith had everything under control. She had a photo shoot in the morning, and she knew she would be good, because she had her little helper in her nightstand drawer. She reached over to double check. It wasn't there! Where could it be? She was certain she had left it there. The only person who saw her take it out was that two-timing low-down creep she was sleeping with. She reached for her phone,

"Slygo, did you take the rest of my stuff?" she demanded. He answered no, but of course she didn't believe him. She hung up the phone in a panic. She needed her stuff. She had to look gorgeous tomorrow, and that's how she did it. Everyone told her she was beautiful. They all thought she was amazing behind the camera lenses. But no one knew how she did it. She had to prep herself, because no matter how much makeup or what breathtaking outfit she wore, she saw trash looking back at her in the mirror. But she was no dummy, and she dared not flaw her skin with needles. She never used more than she needed either. She was in control of this drug. Nothing and no one would control her ever again. She allotted herself the right amount, at the right time, every time. Only then she would be fantastic. Only then she could create magic. It was then that for a moment she too thought she was beautiful. Judith didn't think she had a problem. She always had a little something extra stashed away. She looked on the top shelf of her closet and found her drug. So there—problem solved. She could sleep now. At least that's what she thought.

* * *

Sometimes in life, it's not the boulder in the path that hinders the journey. Those they could see clearly. They can get off the path for a minute and go around it, get back on track. Or they could even climb over. But at times in one's life, the things that do the most damage are those little pebbles and small rocks that they couldn't see in the way. Those were the things that made them misstep and fall. They never saw them in the way, and so therefore there were no problems—until they *became* a problem.

Chapter 13

Her friends all came to see her graduate. She was now a psychologist: Doctor Atylk Summers. They had planned a party that night—an all-night party of course. It had been five years since they had all seen each other, but it might as well have been five days.

They were all still pretty much the same. The only difference was that Shirley had finally gotten married to Trevor. Apparently something had been said at that sleepover years ago that made her realize she needed to be more supportive of her husband, and a little bit more submissive as a wife. Their oldest daughter had graduated from high school. She was a math whiz and could easily calculate the rotation needed to make any machinery her dad made work. She could tell him at what angles two mechanical plates would have to be placed at to touch at the right point, or exactly what measurement a lever would have to be to make anything work. Together with her dad, they had launched a company called Biltwell Products. They made anything, from special furniture pieces and reversible gaming tables to machine dispensers, and their products were often custom-made original pieces. Their customers spent big bucks to get exactly what they wanted. With Shirley's encouragement Trevor was able to turn his passion for fixing and building things around their house into a money-making empire. A look of pride came upon him whenever he got things working around the house, even more so when a part was needed and he improvised, getting the same, if not better results. Shirley knew in her gut that this was what he was meant to do. It was the something she knew she couldn't give him, and she was so proud of him when he found his way. Of course, it meant he spent a little less time with the children and more time away from her, but she trusted him and knew it would only be for a time. When the benefits outweighed the sacrifice, it was all worth it to her. It improved their marriage tremendously and not just in a monetary way. He more was confident and he communicated his fears hopes and dreams with her, which was all she really needed to feel closer to him.

All the children turned out pretty well, actually. Jeff was now a professional football player. There was something about the look his mother gave him and the way she hugged him after his first major game that made him realize that this was what he was going to do. For him it was the sheer thrill of the game, and more than that, it was the first time his mom had said she was proud of him. She had even given him a hug. Sure, she would tell him to give her a hug and a kiss when she visited him at his grandmother's house, and she did call him every night to make sure he did his homework. But that day when he won his game, *she* hugged him back, and for the first time it was all the reassurance he needed that his mom did love him. For the first time, when she looked at him, she really *saw him*.

* * *

Atylk's thoughts drifted back to her daughter, Salo, who was running her own company. Atylk thought back to all the different things Salo wanted to be when she grew up. Atylk was so nervous by the time she was in high school. One week she wanted to be an actress, the next day a musician, a week later a director. But by college she could see clearly that she was determined to graduate, thinking beyond what was expected of her. She didn't worry about what company she would work for—no way—she wasn't going to be an employee; she was determined to be the employer. She had combined her love for poetry and the magic of words—the one thing that stayed constant in her life—with her talent as a Web page designer, which was her gift. She was a smart one, all right. She could have been any of those things she wanted to be in high school, but in the end she opted to work smart and not hard. Everyone sought her out for advertisements. They needed her to help them bring in more money. But for them to generate sales and make more, she would be first on their payroll. So by doing the things she loved she made lots of money, for what she did she did well. Her heart was in it, and in Salo's mind she would never work a day in her life, because she was having fun and getting paid doing it.

Atylk was proud of Salo, right down to the way she carried herself. Gone were the days with the bright-colored wigs, dark eyeliner, and black nail polish. Now, with class and pride and a strong sense of self-worth, her entire demeanor attracted men like moths to a flame. The thugs with their hats turned backwards and their pants falling off their waists didn't waste time looking in Salo's direction. But who would her daughter's husband be? Atylk wasn't quite sure, but it certainly wasn't something she panicked about at all. Today she could say she trusted her judgment.

The jolt of someone jabbing her in her side brought Atylk back to the present. Everyone but her realized it was time to leave. The graduation ceremony was over.

"You guys see what I'm talking about?" Judith was saying. "She hasn't changed a bit. Snap out of it, for goodness' sake."

"For real, Atylk, you've got to stop that crap," Pam confirmed. "Where does your mind run off to? You know what, on second thought, I don't want to know."

"Yeah, and if I hear any of that 'my grandma says' bullshit tonight I promise you I'll knock your teeth so far down your throat your dentist won't be able to retrieve them," Shirley added.

"Well I won't, but just for the record, there ain't nothing my grandma says that's bullshit, I would just have you know, young lady," Atylk responded, mimicking her grandmother's tone.

Shirley pretended to dive towards her in a fit of rage. "Somebody please hold me back, hold me back before I kill this girl." In the end they all group hugged.

By the time they got home that night it was apparent that something was going on with Pam. She wasn't putting down anybody or laughing; in fact, she wasn't saying much at all.

"Whenever you're ready to tell us we're listening," Atylk said to her with a knowing smile.

"Tell you what?" she asked nervously.

"After all we've been through do you really believe we can't see that something's bothering you?" Atylk asked.

"I don't know what you're talking about," she said with a nervous smile.

"If you say so, Pam, whatever," Judith said flippantly.

"I'm divorcing Jason," she blurted out. Everyone stopped what they were doing, turned to look at her, and then sat down.

"We just can't get along, guys. I've tried everything. He still insists it's my fault we can't conceive. He has gained all this weight, and to make matters worse he lost his job. You guys know we've been having money problems, so for him to lose his job was the last straw.

"When did all this happen?" Atylk asked. She remembered getting a call from Jason a few years back, but he promised her he would talk to Pam about it.

"Which one? I don't know. Everything has all been gradual, I guess. But the job thing has been six months now and he's not even looking for one. I'm sorry. There is no excusing him this time. People are talking back home, Atylk, and you know our community is so small. I don't want people thinking I'm married to a thief.

"Wait wait, hold up. Could somebody fill me in on what's been going on here?" Atylk asked. She had been so taken up with her own affairs that she was guilty of not staying in touch with the girls.

"Jason's been accused of embezzling company funds," Judith was quick to inform her.

Atylk immediately felt guilty. "Oh no. This could have all been avoided, don't you think, Pam?"

"What do you mean by that?" Pam asked

"Don't you think you've put Jason in this position to give you the lifestyle you want?" Atylk asked.

"The lifestyle I want or *deserve?*" Pam asked indignantly.

"Okay, deserve," Shirley pretended to agree, frustrated with Pam's self-absorbed notions. "You're missing the point, as usual. I have a coworker who lives in one of those penthouse apartments and I was shocked at the money people pay for them."

"Have you ever asked him what brought this on?" Atylk asked.

"Of course I have. Do you think I'm stupid," she all but shouted.

"No, she's just saying you're not too smart," Judith said, tapping the side of her forehead. They were all so used to her remarks that no one paid her any mind. None but Pam, of course. She glared at Judith, then looked back at Atylk.

"He won't talk to me," she said helplessly.

"Can't say that I blame him. You're not exactly the easiest person to talk to," Judith interjected. Pam rolled her eyes at her.

"But she's right you know, Pam," Shirley added. "When I saw him gaining all that weight, didn't I offer to give you some quick, healthy recipes? What did you tell me? You said he married you knowing you didn't cook."

"Do you seriously mean to tell me that instead of learning to cook to help Jason control his weight, you sat back and let it happen?" Atylk said, furious at her friend right now.

"What the heck is this, gang up on Pam day? He is a grown man. I'm the one whose future is filled with uncertainties here." She stood up suddenly. "My law firm will most likely take the case if it comes to that. I'm the one who's reputation—"

"I, me, my," Judith mocked. "Shut up already."

"Stop telling me to shut up. I've always hated it when you do that." She stormed toward the door.

"Palease, spare me the drama." Judith flipped one hand across her face for effect. "Do make sure the door hits you on the way out."

"Seriously, for once in your life, stop controlling the conversation and listen for a change," Atylk insisted. "Jason has had a problem with gambling."

"And just how would you know that?" She stopped walking to the door and turned, glaring with fire in her eyes at Atylk.

"He asked me for help telling you a long time ago," Atylk went on. "Problem was, I was so busy at the time, I simply told him to talk to you about it. I guess he knew how you'd react, so he thought he would work things out somehow. I didn't want to get involved, so I told him you'd be upset but you loved him enough to fix things. I remember how I felt when Judith tried to interfere with my relationship with Curtis and—"

"Why the heck you gotta go back there now? This isn't about us. It's about this egomaniacal self-absorbed twit right here. You need to loosen up. Maybe then you'll get that stick out your ass and give the man some babies," Judith fired at Pam.

"For goodness sakes, Ju, would you knock it off?" The seriousness in Shirley's tone created a twenty seconds of dead silence. "We're missing the point here. Pam, it's very serious if a man would rather steal, go to jail even, trying to correct a wrong—which I'm pretty sure is what happened here—rather than come home and face his wife's wrath."

"Shirley is right. Divorce is the last thing Jason needs to hear right now. This is the time when he needs you the most. You need to go home and assure that man that you'll be there for him." Atylk continued, "I can't speak for everyone, but I'll be here for you if you need me. Only don't be like Judith."

"Oh for Pete's sake, would you leave me out of this." Judith was the one ready to leave the room this time.

"Why, what did she do?" Shirley asked curiously. Atylk looked at Judith silently seeking for permission to tell.

"Whatever," was all Judith said and flopped down on the couch.

"Remember that time she came to visit me," Atylk began. "Well we were both having a rough time and we agreed to be roommates to save money. She never paid a bill in that apartment, and to top it all off she asked me for a loan and dared to be upset because I wanted to know what she intended to do with it. Can you imagine, upset with me for wanting to know where my own money was going!" She looked over at Judith trying to read her expression to see if she should continue. She didn't seem to care, so Atylk went on.

"Ju, was so deep in debt that she could hardly keep up with paying her rent. She knew I would let her move in. She also knew I would want to know what was going on in her life, and she just didn't want a lecture from me. I tried telling her instant gratification would lead to her destruction, but that just pissed her off. But you guys know how she is; she just didn't want to hear it. In the end she told me what was going on and boy was she glad she did. She was on the verge of bankruptcy and it was all so unnecessary. There were all these designer shoes that she had to have but didn't wear, because she didn't have the right outfit yet, and vice versa. Not to mention the name brand purses and sunglasses still in their boxes, and the jewelry. Every woman needs a designer *something* or the other, but she certainly didn't need fifty pairs of designer shoes. It was ridiculous the things she did, really. She would buy a gift for someone and not give them simply because they had pissed her off that day or week. Then there was the time she decided she needed maid service for her small one bedroom condo, yet cleaned up before the maid came over because she was embarrassed to let the maid see what a mess she had created. It's all laughable now, but it was as if she was living and spending unconsciously.

She tried explaining to me that constantly being photographed meant she could never wear certain things twice. But still I just felt there was a better way. Thing was, when her new friends said they were going shopping and asked her to come, there was no way she could say no. She didn't care if she was maxing out her credit cards each time. It was the price she paid for the career she was in. Apparently the price was far higher than she had anticipated.

In the end I was able to get someone to give her an appraisal of all she had, she was able to sell online and cut her total debt in half. It was a rude awakening but it was all worth it. After we did that, she simply consolidated the rest of her debts and made an easy monthly payment. It was such a relief to have bill collectors stop calling her, and not to jump when her home phone rang. Afterwards, she was so relaxed that she was inspired to start her own business.

Judith smiled a coy smile now after listening to Atylk tell the tale.

"Well, it turned out she didn't lend me the money and I'm glad she didn't. One less debt to worry about," said Judith.

My grandmother always says,

"'Don't never lend more than you can afford to lose.'"

"Atylk, for goodness' sake would you stop with that!" said Shirley.

"Sorry, I couldn't help it. The point is, I ended up having to take another roommate. But seriously, if you need an interest free loan I'm here, Pam. But I worked hard to get it, so I just can't give it away. Deal?" Atylk said.

"Why don't you just put it in writing," Shirley suggested.

"Not a bad idea," Atylk pondered.

"I ... she was just kidding." Both Shirley and Judith grabbed pillows to knock her over. But only the three of them were laughing. Pam's mind was far away. She wondered if she could ever fix the mess she had made of her marriage.

Chapter 14

About six months later Atylk was finally on a plane back home. She hadn't seen her grandmother in six years. They would both be happy to see each other.

It had taken Atylk all that time to realize quite a few things. Life wasn't worth living if you couldn't allow yourself to love, to be vulnerable sometimes. After that day she cried in her kitchen, it was so easy for tears to sting her eyes. She cried about the silliest things: baby photos of Salo, dumb romance movies, even the sight of old couples in the park. It was ridiculous, yet so freeing. It was as if all the pain, hurt, and disappointment of her past was a heavy load that had been lifted from her shoulders. She had no idea what the future held for her, but one thing was certain: this time she would do it God's way and she would not fail.

She had been talking to the right people on the phone back in St. Kitts. She had forwarded funds to get her projects up and running and it was now time to meet the staff who would be working for her.

She had carefully orchestrated a plan that would not only provide much needed services to the people in her country but also bring in enough revenue to keep her non-profit organization, The Unit, running in a way that was self-sufficient. It would be like a well-oiled machine.

With her plans for her building in tow, she was about to step into her destiny. She had thought this thing out for years and by liaising with the prime minister of her country she was not only welcomed to set up her organization, but the government worked diligently with her to make it happen as soon as possible. She had already been forwarded the photos of The Unit as it underwent construction. It was a massive rectangular-shaped two-story building. It would be a place where anyone who was willing to work diligently and honestly could realize otherwise impossible dreams.

The Unit was the only one of its kind on the island. For the children, there was a place to live if they were being abused, and there was also a residence for those who were academically inclined but didn't have the resources. There was no stigma attached to anyone at The Unit; everyone coexisted on a level playing field. Only the staff knew why each individual was there. They signed documents to a vow of secrecy. It was of utmost importance that everyone blended in.

There was a wing for battered women as well. Staff helped them with learning to read, getting a high school diploma, and even getting into college. Scholarships were even provided for those who qualified. The same thing applied to the men, although most men who came in were just regular hard-working men hoping to learn a trade that would bring in extra money to support their families.

Although these things were the function of The Unit, looking at it from the outside, you would never think so. Atylk had designed it to look like a five-star resort: beautiful palm trees and lush green grass with beautiful flowers all around. She wanted that peaceful, tranquil ambiance to infuse The Unit with the same spirit.

The one area closest to her heart, though, was the facility for the children. Most kids got into trouble simply because they wanted to belong. They had so much energy and so many ideas that it was imperative to provide a facility for them to play, showcase their talents, and learn. However, not everyone got a chance to come to The Unit. If you didn't reside there, it was for members only, and you couldn't buy membership. You got in based on merit only. Only the children who were spoken of well by their teachers or trustworthy members of their society were given a pass to visit and use the facilities, with the understanding that it was a privilege to be there, not a right. The rules and code of conduct was something they had to recite upon request. It was Atylk's way of ensuring the children knew with certainty what was expected of them. At the end of the year the board reviewed each case. Three violations and their passes were revoked. No second chances.

There was every activity imaginable for children of all ages— from a basketball court, swimming pool, indoor gym, and kiddy play room with race car games to an auditorium where every week a show would be put on to showcase the children's talent. The auditorium was large and formal enough to rent out for special occasions, like weddings too large for a church.

Yes, she had thought this out long and hard all right. A project of this magnitude needed something that would generate enough income to keep it running. So everything the community didn't have already, The Unit provided. There was a twenty-four hour Laundromat. The only bowling alley on the island was there. There was even an all-night pharmacy/foodmart. Her experience from "Mama's Love" restaurant helped are not only to feed the boarders but but also to establish a drive-thru eatery that was fast becoming the most popular one in town. Every function that was needed to run her organization was in one way or another offered to the public to generate money that would be put back into its continued growth. This wasn't something she could leave to chance, hoping someone volunteered and donated funds. Too many lives depended on it.

The main staff who would be working there had no titles except to designate their gender. Mr. James over in marketing or Ms. Sutton in human resources was all anyone was known as. There was no room for titles here. This was a job of services, no one person's job was more important than the other. Thus no titles were given to create any air of superiority. On paper, everyone knew who they were, on paper their titles reflected in their wallets, for Atylk knew that when asked by friends they would have to respond, "I work at The Unit," and say nothing more. For that alone she ensured they were paid handsomely. No one knew she was funding this project except those who had to know. She was just another worker—the psychologist—and that was perfect in Atylk's mind. This wasn't about her; rather, it was about the children and the men and women who needed help but had no place to turn to.

An exercise Atylk did with the staff later that month emphasized the importance of the children's wellbeing. They were asked to complete a simple task, but one of utmost importance. They had to all stand in a line and pass a message to the first person to the right. She started the process by whispering to the person first in line,

"The children need spiritual guidance now, if we hope to have a better tomorrow." As she watched the message being passed she could see some giggling and some confusion, and she knew the message had since been changed. To make her point even more graphic, and to show them how serious she took this assignment, she went through the line to see where the chain in the message was broken. She added another element to the exercise. The first person in line was handed a life-sized baby doll. If the message was passed incorrectly, she would rip a body part away.

She knew the first person got the message right. She told them. So, she asked the second person,

"What did he tell you?"

He stated, "The children need guidance now, to have a better tomorrow."

Atylk looked the first person in line; Mr. James, took the doll away, clenched her teeth and said, "Wrong!" As she said it she tore an arm away from the doll.

The second person passed the message correctly. For that, she reattached the doll's arm, cradled the doll like a real baby, and handed it back over to the second person so he could do the honor of passing it to the next person in line. However, by the time the message got to the fifth person, the message was now, "The chicken needs guidelines, to bet on tomorrow." In the end, only the doll's torso and head was all that was left, and the last person in line *still* received an incorrect message. Atylk then pressed a button and the initial message popped up on the screen. She ended by saying to them, "Ladies and gentlemen, let us pretend for a minute this was a real child counting on us to carry out our task. Is this how we would fail them? For today only, I can commend those who listened carefully and relayed the message. But had this been a real-life exercise it wouldn't matter. No matter how sincere your intentions, the fact is you were delivered a wrong message. You were left with no other choice but to deliver that incorrect message. That fact in and of itself is a major problem. Let's never take anything we're doing at The Unit for granted please. Life is not this forgiving. At the end of the day, teaching the wrong thing can't become right. No matter how hard you try. This, *this*, is the result of us failing our children, generation after generation. *Look at it*," Atylk insisted, holding up the limbless, hairless torso of the doll. "There is nothing left now for me to detach, yet I must. Should I tear its heart out, or maybe rip its neck off?" She lifted her chin and raised an eyebrow. She could see by the somber look on their faces that she had gotten her point across. "This is someone's child we've just destroyed, people. I beg of you, take each and every assignment given to you at The Unit seriously. Take it to heart. Were done for today."

Atylk left that meeting feeling a bit disappointed. However, there was something else of grave importance she had to do that day. She pulled herself together and headed off to Washing High School to recruit a guidance counselor—a male counselor. She realized she desperately needed one for The Unit.

The following week her cousin Madeline would be coming back home too. She had moved to America to live with her dad in order to finish college. Madeline was always fascinated with the way their grandmother could brew a tea for any ailment, or to strengthen her body's weaknesses. Madeline ultimately became a pharmacist and was coming home to head the pharmacy division of The Unit.

That night there was a party to celebrate her grandmother's ninety-ninth birthday. Atylk's mom and her brother and sister were there. Her aunt, Madeline's mom, was also there. It was like a reunion of sorts. Some folks gave short speeches about the role she played in their lives. Others thanked her for the freedom they had to call her up early and ask about a dream they had. Many thanked her for the great meals she prepared. The affection everyone had for her was apparent even in the way they said her name. They all called her Aunt Isa—pronouncing it as one word, "Auntisa"—even though she wasn't their aunt. Among friends, everyone laughed and talked about their past, their struggles, and their breakthroughs.

As for Atylk, she looked around the room and saw her girlfriends from her childhood with their families and she realized one thing. As a child, she had read all these books. However, no matter what books one reads, what lectures one hears, or what advice to get from friends, everyone must find the courage to do what needs to be done. Looking around the room now, she just saw children. No matter how old they had gotten, that's all they were. Some hid behind masks of insecurity, defining who they were by their jobs. Others obsessed about how they looked on the outside—their size and their clothes. Others measured their worth by what they had. Yet they were all pretty much the same. They all had a story, they all had issues, they all had to fall and get up at some point in life. No one could measure the depth of pain the other person felt, because they all dealt with their pain differently. But they were just children in her eyes.

Was it not childish for her to let uncertainty about the future make her not take one step into a territory she feared most? Wasn't it childish for them to gamble their life savings away? Or worse yet, to spend more than they earned in the hopes that things would be better tomorrow? Wasn't it childish, when blessed with a healthy body to overeat, get *un*healthy, and then pray for a miracle? Or to abuse substances with the rationale that they could quit whenever they wanted? Or perhaps worst of all, to think they were so perfect and did everything right to the point where no one wanted to be around them? Yes. For sure they all had things they needed to fix and they all knew it. What they lacked was the will to do it.

That night it occurred to Atylk what she needed to do for Judith, and for herself as well. She knew she would have a hard time convincing Judith to go, but it was worth a try. She called Judith first to let her know of her plans and while she didn't quite say yes, she didn't say no either. She made an appointment with a therapist for both of them to go in together. It was quite pricy in Atylk's opinion, but she was willing to pay it simply because she liked the way Dr. Solomon conducted his sessions. Each patient had a choice—draw two paintings, write two poems or letters, or simply talk. One had to be of their happiest moment and one of their saddest moment in life. They would break for lunch, come back, and with the help of Dr. Solomon somehow connect these two moments in life. They booked him for the entire day. Knowing Judith it would take them two days, Atylk thought.

The next morning Atylk showed up at Judith's door to pick her up as scheduled. Atylk knocked and was greeted by silence. She had a key, so let herself in Judith's condo. As she walked through the house she realized that things were much worse than she had thought. Judith's pain was evident all over her condo. Here entire living room set was covered with bags upon bags of items she had recently bought. As she passed the kitchen she noticed the sink was full and overflowing with dishes. Atylk would definitely be telling her about this; she had a dishwasher, so there was no excuse for such a mess. There was a terrible stench coming from the dining room. As Atylk approached she saw the leftover sushi on the table. It reeked in a way that told her it was from days before. Just by looking around, Atylk could diagnose her friend's problems right away, but she decided not to say anything, knowing Judith would get defensive and say that she was judging her.

Atylk herself had times in her younger years when the local television channel signed off at midnight and sleep still wouldn't come to her eyes. She would just stare at the vertical colored lines on the screen, and as the television buzzed on her mind would wander off. She would daydream about what it would be like to be in a normal family. She pictured in a family with both her mom and dad and herself walking on the beach; one would hold her left arm the other her right, swinging her back and forth. She knew she could never have that, and it made her heart ache as if someone was trying to twist it until it broke apart. A lump would form in her throat, and for hours she would just stare at the TV until exhaustion overtook her and she fell asleep, only to dream of happy times with a family she wished she could have. Often times she woke up feeling guilty, because she knew her grandmother loved her and tried her very best to ensure she had everything she needed. But she didn't want material things; she wanted her mom and her dad. Yes, she certainly wouldn't judge her friend, because she too had the same pain—the pain of absent parents. But there was no way to convince Judith of that.

Atylk walked tentatively to her friend's bedroom and knocked softly before pushing the door open. What she saw was both shocking and disturbing. Judith was wrapped up in a blanket, fast asleep. (Or at least that's what she wanted Atylk to believe.) On the dressing table, at the foot of her bed, and on the floor were shoes clothes and purses everywhere. Her friend was never really a neat freak, but she always at the very least pushed her stuff in her closet until she found inspiration to sort them out and even give some away if she was in a good mood. They had both laughed the first time Atylk opened her closet and everything came tumbling down.

Most shockingly, these weren't just regular T-shirts and jeans on the floor. Everything was a designer label. From Prada purses and Michael Kors belts to Jimmy Choo shoes and Gucci sunglasses. She even had a Burberry Prorsum dress just lying there in the middle of the floor. You would think after spending all this money on them she would take better care of them. All this told Atylk that her intervention was indeed timely, that there was a lot more going on with her friend than she was letting on. It was like déjà vu. Atylk thought that her friend had long ago gotten over her obsession with shopping. Atylk knew she had to approach this situation with the utmost care.

"Ju, it's time to wake up honey," Atylk said softly, gently shaking her. "We have a nine o'clock appointment and it's already after eight."

"Mmmmm, I told you I didn't want to go. How did you get in here anyway?" she mumbled as she rolled over and pulled herself into a fetal position while covering her head with the blanket.

"You gave me a key when you first got this place, remember?" Atylk answered.

"Oh yeah, how dumb was that? I had a sleepless night and I was just getting some sleep finally when you came barging in here." Judith was trying to sound tough, but Atylk knew it was just a cover-up. "Can we do this some other time?"

"No, we can't. Dr. Solomon cancelled his appointment for today just to fit us in. It would be so impolite of us to cancel on him. Come on, babes, I'll help you get ready." Atylk tried to be patient instead of arguing with her friend for not being ready. However, her efforts threatened to backfire. She threw back the covers and started yelling.

"Why the hell are you being so nice? Don't come up in here with that psycho bullshit. You know how I hate it. What! What is it? What do you want from me?" Her tirade was accompanied by a wild look in her eyes that would have deterred another person, but Atylk knew it was just a lot of barking and nothing else. "Do you want me to tell you how sad and disappointed I am that Daddy Dearest didn't give a shit if I had dinner? Or how hurt I was that he never called after a month of leaving us? Maybe I should go ahead and tell you that I have slept with sooo many guys I've lost count. Since that son of a bitch raped me, do you think I care? Aside from Jeff I don't give a shit about any male. Any! Do you hear me? Do you hear me!" She was screaming now, and Atylk's look of concern wasn't helping. Atylk had long gotten over being alarmed at the way Judith expressed herself. She knew Judith did it deliberately for shock value. Sometimes it seemed like her words oozed venom. "Don't. D-d-don't! Don't you dare do that!" She was swaying her hands vigorously back and forth in from of her face, while shaking her head from left to right. She looked like a caged animal.

"Don't what?" Atylk asked.

"You don't have to say it. I know what you're thinking. Oh poor Judith. I feel so sorry for her," she said mockingly. "I hate that shit. Sorry doesn't fix anything, what's done is done and guess what? I don't want your pity! I want you the leave me the hell alone, because you're clueless right now." With that she tried to scurry off the bed, but Atylk wouldn't let her leave. She knew her friend too well. There was more going on here.

"Judith, did something else happen? Did someone try to hurt you?" Atylk asked, anxiously searching her friend's eyes. Then Judith did something Atylk had never seen her do: she began to laugh and cry at the same time.

"So, the great Dr. Atylk can't figure this one out, can she? Can't you tell by the tone of my voice? Look deep, Atylk. Look deep into my eyes. Nothing? Give up? I'll tell you." She paused for a minute, wiping her eyes with the back of her hands.

Atylk wondered if this had anything to do with the phone call she had received from John. John was her manager and was ten years her senior. Atylk always suspected he cared for Judith more than he let on, because he was always rescuing her. He helped her pay her rent and took her home when she was too drunk to drive. But he never told anyone how he really felt about Judith.

"Does this have anything to do with John?" Atylk asked.

"How'd you figure that?"

"I really think he cares about you, Ju."

"Cares about me, huh?" Her lips turned down in an upside-down smile as she asked herself the question. "So is that why he walked out on me after I threw myself at him? Can't say that I blame him. He's watched me go out with every Tom, Dick, and Harry." She sat on the bed with her knees pulled up to her face and rested her head there while she hugged her ankles. There was such a sad, faraway look on her face that Atylk just wanted to hug her. Of course she knew she couldn't—it would only make Judith mad. That was how she remained as she told Atylk the tale of what happened with John a few nights earlier.

"Instead of tucking me in and leaving like he always does, he told me it was killing him to see me throw myself away like I do. He started talking like he was my father, telling me I needed to make up my mind about who I wanted to be with and stick to it. Blah, blah, blah. You know what the worst part is? I threw myself at him and he rejected me."

Judith relived what happened in her mind, and she tried her best to relay the tale of what happened last week to Atylk.

As it turned out, John dropped her off and was about to leave as usual, but his heart ached so much for this woman he had grown to love, he couldn't help himself. He kissed her on the cheek. He thought he would just leave after that. But Judith slipped her fingers around his neck and pulled his lips to hers. It was like all the nights he had gone to bed dreaming about her were combined in this one intense moment. She kissed him as if she was desperate for his touch. Could he be imagining this? He thought he saw desire in her eyes when their kiss finally ended. But he knew he needed this woman to want him and not just another tumble under the sheets. He made another attempt to leave, and she pleaded in a husky tone, "Don't go. I need you." At that point he couldn't leave even if he wanted to. He kissed her as if he were a man drowning and only this woman's loving could save him.

"Open your eyes baby. I need you to look at me." It wasn't a command but rather a desperate plea that Judith thought she understood. As she opened her eyes and looked into the depth of his, he said, "I love you, Judith. I've loved you from the day you walked into my office." She heard him, and his words echoed in her head. They seemed to move though her body and settle in a place deep within her and made her feel warm all over. "I love you too much to just be a number on your list. Make no mistake, I want you, but not like this. If you think you can commit to loving me and only me,

I'll be waiting. I need your heart, not just your body. I need a wife, not a quick fix." And just like that, he left.

His words seemed to pour cold water all over her. Was he telling her she wasn't good enough for him? She was more confused now than ever. She fell asleep feeling sad that it had taken her this long to see how much this man cared about her. Was it was too late? Was he telling her she wasn't wife worthy? He too fell asleep feeling sad, because he was clueless as to whether or not she loved him back.

As she finished telling her friend what had happened to her, Atylk asked, "So, do you love him?"

A fresh wave of tears poured from her eyes. "Of course I do. I've always had just sex with the guys I've been with. I never cared before. John makes me care. John, he makes me feel things I would rather keep locked up, and when he said he loved me, I believed him … I really did."

"Have you told him?" Atylk prodded.

"No, what's the point. Weren't you listening? He said he wanted a wife, Atylk. That kind of excludes me, right? I haven't called or seen him since. I'm too scared to answer his phone calls."

"You have to call him, Ju."

"Stop telling me what to do!" she screamed, pulling the blanket back over her head lying back in the bed. Atylk knew she was treading on delicate waters.

"I'm not telling you what to do, Ju. I'm just asking you to think about his feelings for a change. We both know what it feels like to want to be loved and not get it. It's the most heart-wrenching feeling ever. Just try to be brave and call him ask him to come over. I can tell he loves you very much. He'll understand why you haven't called. He won't judge you."

Atylk knew that being judged was one of Judith's biggest fears.

"How the heck would you know?"

"Because, silly, if he thought less of you after seeing you date every Tom, Dick, and Harry, as you put it, he wouldn't have opened his heart to you like that," she said with certainty.

"What makes you so sure?" she said, peeking out from under the covers.

"Because, silly, I see male patients almost every day. You think it's scary for us to open up? You have no idea how hard it is for them." Atylk stood up and started cleaning up. What she didn't tell her friend was that John had called her and told her he cared deeply about Judith. He wanted to marry her, protect her from the world. It was very tricky trying to deal with Judith though. She simply told him to be patient and assured him she'd come around. It was a leap of faith, one that Judith needed to take of her own free will. "Here, I'll help you clean up."

"What about our appointment?" Judith asked.

"It's okay. I won't force you if you don't want to."

"I think I want to go," she said softly.

Atylk held her hands. "Okay. But I want you to do something for me first. Watch my fingers and count with me to ten in your mind." Judith rolled her eyes, but she did it anyway. But before they got to ten Atylk said, "Now say, 'I am fearfully and wonderfully made.'"

Judith recited, "I am fearfully and wonderfully made."

"Now, see how you had all that negative energy when I asked you to count? You just need to replace that with some positive energy by speaking well of yourself out loud. When those thoughts come to your head, just say out loud, 'I'm beautiful,' and soon you'll start to believe it."

"Okay, whatever you say, Atylk," she let out a long breath.

"Promise me," Atylk insisted and waited until Judith nodded yes. "Okay, go get ready. I'll fix up."

When they got to Dr. Solomon's office both girls drew a picture of their happiest moment. They couldn't see what the other drew, but when they came together it was so hilarious to them that they both drew pictures of themselves as little girls playing on the beach with their friends. It was a time in their lives when they were young and innocent to the hardships of life. It was a time when life was full of promise.

For their saddest moments, again they had the same idea. They both wrote about their dads, only Atylk wrote a poem and Judith wrote a love letter to her father.

Judith's love letter read,

> *It's been 2 months since you left, Dad. I hope you're alright. You haven't called at all this month Dad. I wish you didn't have to go. I wish there was more I could do. Mom cries herself to sleep at night when she thinks we're sleeping. I wish I could talk to you. I wish I could tell you to come back home. I don't want the things your money will buy. Instead I need your hugs at night. I promise with my help we could make it together as a family. I'm old enough now, I could do a part-time job on the weekends to help with the bills. I could look out for Leslie and Tom, make dinner until Mom gets home if she got a job too. I promise Dad, I'll be the best daughter ever. You'll be so proud of me, I just want you home Dad. We need you. Who's gonna teach Tom how to be a man. Who's gonna punish me for staying on the phone too long*

or staying out with a boy too late. Who's going to tell me what to expect from guys who want nothing more than a good time in bed? Who's gonna walk me down the aisle when I get married? We have an uncle living with us, but he's nothing like you. ~~Actually I don't like him, I don't like him one bit ... I wish you were here to protect me, cuz I don't like the way he looks at me.~~

Judith didn't like where this was going. She crumpled up her paper and was about to throw it in the garbage when Atylk took it from her. As Atylk read it aloud, Judith started to cry again. Atylk thought maybe she was opening old wounds, but what Judith didn't mention was that this was an actual letter she wrote to her dad years ago, only she had no address to mail it to.

To make her feel that she wasn't alone in this, Atylk read her poem. It read,

My Dream Dad

I dream of you quite often Dad, and it often makes me quite sad. For in my dreams you're always my hero, but I always wake up to tomorrow. When I wake you're not there.

I dream of you almost every night. You're always there to hold me tight. You're there to celebrate my accomplishments big and small, but I wake to find out you're not there at all.

I dream that you're there to pick me up when I fall off my bike. You pick me up and tell me it will be all right. I wake, wishing you were here.

I dream about you a lot Dad, and although you are not perfect you can do no wrong. Your strength for staying with me when other dads leave, in turn makes me feel strong.

I'm tired of dreaming Dad, if only you would just call. I'm tired of dreaming Dad, I need to know you're out there ... somewhere, thinking about me. Wishing you could be there for me. I need to connect with you somehow Dad. Send a card, a letter, I don't want money.

I won't be like other children, I won't complain about what I don't have. I will love you just for being there. I will love you just by knowing you care.

Can I just hear you voice for my birthday, or Christmas maybe? I don't even care about the tree. I just want to wake up and see you smiling at me. If only I could just have your voice to comfort me...

Atylk couldn't get through her poem either, because they were both crying like little girls, but by the time they took a break for lunch, they both felt like a weight had been lifted from their shoulders. When they regrouped, they talked about how relieved they felt after getting in touch with their feelings. Dr. Solomon helped them both find a way to see how, even though they didn't have their dads around, they should both be proud of how far they had come. He told them that not having a father shouldn't hold them back. Judith would do the same thing to her son, if she wasn't careful. He was now twenty-one and living with her as they sought to fix the rift between them. She was there for him physically but so far away emotionally.

As for Atylk, she was so worried about being strong enough to get things done that she locked out anyone who wanted to partner with her. But more importantly, both women had finally forgiven their dads, so they didn't have to carry that pain around anymore.

They were both given a picture frame as a gift at the end of the session. When they got to their homes and tore the gift wrapping paper off, it was a photo of a child being held in the arms of Jesus, and a scripture taken from 1 John 4:4. The picture of Jesus was only his silhouette, and although it was transparent, with only the child showing up in color, there was something about it that spoke to Atylk's soul. It was as if He was saying, "Even though you can't see me, I'm here." Atylk was so moved that she grabbed her Bible and read the entire chapter.

Chapter 15

Everything she had ever wished for and prayed about had come to pass. Atylk had long given up any hopes of ever getting married, and so she remained focused on the children in her organization. But pray she had, and in her prayers, when no one could hear her and it was only just her and her Heavenly father, she confessed. She confessed that she had sinned and begged for forgiveness. But she *also* confessed that if she could have her way, she *would* like to have a man in her life. A man who would love her like no other man had ever loved a woman, but still able to love and revere the Lord. A man who understood her needs without her having to say them. A man who would never, ever let her down. In her darkest moments, when she was too exhausted to face another day, she prayed that he was there to tell her, "Rest a while, baby. I got you." She prayed, "Lord, even if I can't be with him right away, at least let me meet him, please. Just so that I know he is there."

But indeed she had met him. She didn't bump in to him someplace, and she certainly wasn't going to let her friends set her up. The only one she trusted with a venture of this nature was her Heavenly Father, and boy did he *set her up*. You see, he was right there all along, and she was right there all along, yet they never saw each other—at least not in that way. You see, she and this man fought tooth and nail, the way Pam and Judith fought. So they had long ago deemed their relationship "unhealthy," for no matter what it was or how simple it was, they fought about everything. Her friend just assumed they had a love-hate relationship as kids. As teenagers their personalities clashed even more. She was a born leader, and he thought he knew everything. If she was texting her friends and he was hovering over her he would say, "The time it takes you to go get the '&' sign you could have typed the word 'and.'"

She hated when he told her what to do, so she would then respond, "Why don't you just *ask* me why I use it instead of putting your nose where it doesn't belong? I'm trying to save space in my text message, if you must know."

Of course that wasn't true. She only typed more information in her message to prove him wrong. They cared about each other a lot indeed, but what they lacked was the maturity that was needed to be kind, to have faith and hope, and not to be puffed up. By the time they became adults he would say, "Why are you always reading those dumb romance novels?"

"Because I want to. You got a problem with that?"

"Don't tell me you believe in that 'happily ever after' crap? Nothing lasts forever—nothing!"

Naturally, she gave as good as she got.

"Is *that* why you bring a new girl over every weekend?"

"I don't bring them. They come."

"Only a weak man … has difficulty saying no."

Yep, they fought a lot all right. But secretly she wished he would stop picking on her. He had turned into quite a hunk. All the girls wanted to be his. They would drop whoever they were with for a chance to be with him. That included Atylk, but he never asked her out. Pride would not allow her to admit she cared about him. At least not to him.

Secretly he wished she would give him the time of day. She would probably break his heart anyway. All women are cheaters. His mom was married to his dad for twenty years, then ran off with another man when he turned eighteen. If that didn't prove that women were cold-hearted, nothing would.

But life had taken them full circle, and coming back home awakened old and new feelings within them. But no matter what skills she had, it was hard for the boys at The Unit to open up with her. David Rose was a counselor at the largest high school in the city. She hired him to work at The Unit against her better judgment. This was the same David who pulled her hair as a child, bullied her as a teenager, and tried to make her think she was ignorant to the realities of life as an adult. But she hired him because he was the only male counselor with that much experience dealing with troubled teenagers and who was also a Christian. For that reason alone she had no choice. She had to hire him, because sharing the same belief system was extremely important to her when dealing with the children.

Atylk had walked into David's office with determination. She wasn't going to let him rattle her nerves. She was a grown woman now and she wasn't about to let him get to her the way he did when they were children. However, when he came to the door of his office to escort her in, his looks disarmed her. She wanted to turn and run. She almost did too. But she knew she couldn't she had to do this. For the children she had to face this man. But all she could think of, was wine. Fine aged wine. David Rose had gotten sexier with age. He still had that chiseled body. But more than that his features drew her in like a bee to a hive. His lips looked surprisingly soft for a man, and Atylk found that she couldn't look away. But his smile was the thing that made her knees go weak. His smile reached his eyes with a sincerity she had never noticed in him before. They glistened and Atylk was transfixed with the man who stood before her.

She tried her best to gather her composure and prayed her legs wouldn't betray her as she tried not to wobble to the seat he motioned to. Satisfied that she made it, she smiled and they exchanged pleasantries as they sought to catch up on what they'd been up to in the past few years. It was merely a formality, because Judith was the mediator between them both. They "casually" liaised with Judith in an attempt to keep abreast of what was happening in the other's life. They were both too stubborn to admit to each other that they cared.

Their conversation turned serious as she explained the function of The Unit and why she felt she needed him on board. He didn't commit fully, because he said the students he worked with now needed him. However, he did promise to help out as much as he could. He said he would transition to a full-time position if and when that was necessary. Atylk was so impressed with the man that sat before her. She had studied the files that her human resource manager brought her with possible candidates for this position, and no one else had such an impressive record of getting through to teens like David Rose.

His methods were unconventional, but that was always the way he was. He was the kind of man that did things his way and didn't care what you thought about it—he just got the job done. Other guidance counselors did their work like a job, talking to the students from the comfort of their office. But David Rose worked with passion. He visited students' homes, met their parents, and worked tirelessly to remove students from bad environments when necessary. It was a difficult thing to do. Their society was so small that adoption was unheard of and it took a lot for new family to take in a child that wasn't coming into their homes as a toddler or a baby. No one knew it, but if he couldn't get them a part-time job he often used his own money to ensure such students had food at home and all the school supplies they needed.

The first time David did show up for the staff meeting at The Unit, he was awfully quiet. By the time the meeting ended he asked to see her in her office.

"So what can I do for you, Mr. Rose?" she asked, motioning for him to sit as the both entered the office.

"When, did I become Mr. Rose for you, Atylk?" David asked seriously.

She smiled, tilted her head to one side, and put both palms up to face him. She tried to sound bubbly and cheerful. "I meant no harm. Just trying to keep it professional."

He sat in the chair she motioned to, but as she tried to move around the desk he stopped her dead in her tracks.

"Come here, Atylk," he said softly, beckoning her with his index finger. She couldn't help but obey. He tapped his thigh as if wanting her to sit there. She stood frozen from the shoulders down and shook her head side to side, saying no. He slouched in his chair and said, "Please."

There was something different about this David. The old David would have simply closed the door behind them and trapped her between both arms if he wanted to make a move on her. He never made unwanted advances against the women he dated. He simply oozed sensuality and made *them* fall over him. He had worked up quite a reputation. But this David seemed oddly relaxed, comfortable in his own skin. This David somehow made her feel at ease, and trusting somehow. She did as he asked and sat on his thigh. He remained in that slouched position and asked her in the calmest manner, "When you left and moved to St. Thomas, why didn't you care enough to tell me you were leaving?"

"I don't know. I didn't think you cared one way or the other," Atylk replied. He put his head back, ran both hands down his face, and let out a deep breath. "Why does it matter now anyway?" she asked. He sat forward slowly. His face was so close to hers that when he spoke his breath caressed her face. Atylk held his gazed as he said,

"You're right. What matters now is that you're here now." That wasn't what she meant, but okay.

"Listen, I've never been a man of many words, so I don't care to impress you with charm talk, 'Your eyes are bright like the morning's light' and all that crap. I get straight to the point." Atylk wondered where he was going with this. "What I can tell you is that I'm a good man. Not a perfect man, but a good man. Given the chance, I can promise you this: I can promise you I'll be the best man you ever had and all the man you'll ever need."

"Wait, wait, hold up," Atylk interrupted.

"That's just it—I don't want to wait. You've had had me waiting quite a few years, Ms. Summers. I've prayed for this and I can only do my part in letting you know how I feel. The rest is up to you."

"What makes you think we'll be good together?" Atylk's emotions were on a rollercoaster at this point.

"That depends on what you mean by 'good together.'" He raised both eyebrows and gave her a coy smile.

"I *meant* we never got along before. What makes you think we'll get along now?"

"Here's the deal. Most people connect on two of a possible seven levels—*physically* and *sexually*—and that's not going to last if you want to have a meaningful relationship. I think we're at a place in life where we have a shot at all seven. We know each other's educational background so we're good *intellectually*." Atylk felt like she was in school, but she listened anyway. "I think you can hold your own in a *social* situation and not embarrass me." He laughed at the outraged expression she tried to portray. "And am I not doing a good job of connecting with you *emotionally*? It might not be politically correct, but it's *my* way of talking and opening up with you. And it took me quite a while to get here, I might add. Concerning your *financial* security, I am by no means a rich man, but I have enough invested to make you comfortable. But I think the thing that's at the top of both of our list is our *spiritual* connection. It's been a long journey for me, Atylk, but I think I'm finally at the place God wants me to be. I know the purpose he has for my life. I look at the work you're doing here, and it warms my heart to see that we have the same vision." He looked at her with such intensity it was as if he was seeing her soul. "I'm proud of you, Atylk." He said it so softly that her heart filled up.

"I'm proud of you too, David." She couldn't help it; she leaned in and kissed him. He returned the kiss with as much if not more fervor than she gave it.

When it finally ended, he rested his forehead against hers and said,

"I gotta tell you though, before any of this, I'm a just a man. So let's get back to the first two. *Physically* you're a sight to behold. And dog gone it, I can speak for both of us when I say we definitely connect *sexually*."

She kept her forehead to his and asked with a hint of laughter, "What makes you think you can speak for me?"

"Actually, *I'm* not. Our bodies are." She looked down to see what he was looking at and jumped off his thigh.

"David!" she shouted, pulling her blazer over her bosom to hide what he had detected.

"I'm sorry. I didn't mean to embarrass you, but you asked," he said, smiling from ear to ear. "You should know by now not to ask me a question if you don't want an honest answer. I don't know any other way to be." She was smiling too, but pointed to the door, indicating he should leave. "Seriously, think about it. I really thought you knew I loved you, Atylk."

"How could I? You were always so mean to me," she said, shrugging her shoulders.

"That was just because I thought you were playing hard to get, and it frustrated the heck out of me. I was young. I just didn't know how to deal with it. We've got no one to blame but ourselves for all the time we've wasted. But the ball is in your court. I'm ready and waiting for you to meet me halfway on this. I've got to know you want me as badly as I want you."

As he walked to the door, she smiled, touched her cheeks with both hands, and took a deep breath. She exhaled, wondering why he never asked if she loved him back. David Rose made her feel so many emotions all at once. He could turn her into a nervous wreck, make her as happy as she could possibly be, excite her like a blushing teenager, all at the same time. Yes, he knew she loved him all right. She shook her head at the arrogance of this man. But oddly, it was that very arrogance that she found most appealing about him. He was confident in the man he was and he knew the woman she was. The sheer maleness of him cried out to and awakened everything that was female within her.

So Atylk thought about it and in no time it seemed they were walking down the aisle. But they both wondered if getting married so quickly before ironing out the things they did that made them get so flustered with each other would be their downfall. Their first six months of marriage were indeed difficult. Not because they didn't love each other—they loved each other intensely—but because they fought just as intensely. She had to tell him everything when they got engaged. Not just that The Unit was her project but also that she was rich. He wanted to quit, because he didn't want to risk ruining their personal relationship with a business relationship. She couldn't *let* him, of course, so she promised to be the most obedient wife there ever was. Soon Atylk learned to be submissive, but Lord knows it took all the faith and patience she could muster.

David was sure to let her know when they got engaged, "Let's get this clear. I don't work *for* you. I am working *with* you. I don't want you thinking you can boss me around."

"Why do you think I would do that?" she asked in her sweetest, most angelic voice.

"Don't try that voice on me. I know you," he responded.

"Just like I know you," she cooed, leaning in to kiss him tenderly on the lips.

An obedient wife she was, and she loved every minute of it.

She liked it when he told her what sexy outfit she should wear to bed—especially when he texted her earlier in the day. It made her anticipate the evening to come. Sometimes he would follow it up with a voice message telling her every single detail of how he would make love to her when they got home. Sure enough, he was a man of his word and did his husbandly duties right down to the tiniest details he had outlined to her earlier.

No matter how much he wanted her, he never rushed. They had a lifetime to spend together. He distinctly remembered one evening when she begged him to make love to her. He quite liked it when she begged. There was something about the huskiness in her voice that told him she wanted and needed him. As he placed featherlike kisses all over her body, he found every hidden crevice to plant his kisses. The sounds of her moans turned what was first a soft tender kiss into a kiss of urgency and intense passion. He wanted this woman like no other, and he loved her. He loved her lips, her hips. Her whole body was like a fine work of art, and he felt like the luckiest man alive to be blessed with the honor of enjoying this artwork his Heavenly Father sculpted just for him. He wasn't selfish; he knew she wanted to enjoy him too, and as she returned the favor and touched and kissed him all over he quickly took charge again before he broke his vow to make this magic last as long as humanly possible. As he joined his body to hers, the sounds of pleasure escaping her lips, combined with the rhythm her hips made, threatened to undo him. He held her hips firmly in place so she could experience the magic, while he remained rock solid and ready to do it all over again. David, being the man he was, was sure to let her know that too.

"Did that feel good?" he asked as his lips nibbled her ear. She had no words, so she simply shook her head to say yes while holding on to his wide shoulders. "Good. You'll do that four more times for me before we're done." There was something about that take charge nature about him that brought her to heights of ecstasy like she had never experienced.

By the end of the night she felt like she had not only tasted a glimpse of heaven four more times, but a fifth time along with him. As their bodies did a frenzied dance of desperation she held on to him like she never wanted to let him go. She was exhausted, yet she didn't want it to end. He touched her in places she didn't know she had, both on her body and in her heart. That's why *this* night she refused to let him break their bodies apart. She rode the waves of their love like an expert surfer, and when she collapsed she knew she was safe. For his arms embraced her with such love and tenderness that she cried, her body shuddering.

"I got you, baby. I got you."

That's how they stayed, connected, holding on to each other as they fell asleep. Their sleep lasted only a half hour, the sensation of kisses on her eyes, ear, nose, and lips awakened her to the joyous feel of her man's love for her. As she felt his love for her rise deep within her, he felt fresh waves of love pour over him. For a minute before he fell asleep he was upset that she did what she did, but he discarded the thought when he realized how selfish he was. They both wanted a child together, but for the past six months he was enjoying the pleasures of his wife's love every night and didn't want to interrupt that pattern, not even for a baby. Yes, he loved Atylk Summers Rose. Even when they fought, she still aroused him. He remembered their first fight as husband and wife.

"Babes, I see you forgot to pay the electricity bill, so I did it this morning," she said, flipping through the mail before placing the bills on the desk.

"I paid it already, dear. What bill did you pay?" he asked, getting flustered.

"The most recent one. I thought you forgot to pay it when I saw two months had accumulated," she said defensively.

"Didn't we talk about this? We agreed I would do the bills and you would take care of the groceries. I was trying to sort out a discrepancy with them and they were supposed to get back to me. That's probably why the other month was added."

"I was only trying to help!"

"So why didn't you just ask me?"

"It doesn't matter, babes. We would still need to pay it."

"That's not the point. We could have used that money for something else."

"It's not like we're broke, David."

"You know what your problem is?" he said while walking to their bedroom. He was pulling out all her trousers from the closet and throwing them on the floor.

"What in the world are you doing?"

"Something I should have done a long time ago. Listen here and listen good. There is only room enough for one man around here. From now on you're not wearing any pants unless it's something short and sexy around the house." He followed up by throwing her belts on the pile as well.

"Are you crazy?"

"Not yet, but you're taking me there." He came back to face her. "You've been taking care of yourself for so long that you can't let go and trust me to do it." She was about to open her mouth in protest when he clenched his teeth, put his hand on his hip with legs wide open, and said, "No pants!" The glare he was giving her dared her to argue.

"Okay, okay, no pants," she conceded. As soon as he relaxed she added, "But only women put their hands on their hips." She had to run after that, but of course he caught her and took her to their bed and proved to her he was in fact all man.

Yes he loved Mrs. Rose all right. The way her nostrils flared when she was upset, the way she would lift her chin in defiance—it was all such a turn on for him. This little woman dared to defy him. Not that would ever hurt a hair on her head, but boy she tested him. Looking at her now, he knew she was meant to be a Rose. Her lips parted like a flower opening to the morning sun. He kissed them again but only a few seconds. As a moan of protest escaped her lips, he molded his lips back to hers. Her kisses wreaked havoc on his senses. He didn't care about his ego right now. Tomorrow he would think about how this little woman, with her wild hips, curious hands, and sensuous legs rubbing the back of his like a cat in heat could bring him to such a state of arousal. But right now, an army couldn't get him off her. Her touch, her smell, it was all so intoxicating that in no time, it was over for him. As his body shuddered, *he* was now holding on to her as if his next breath depended on it. As she met him right there right at that place where the magic of love happens, they were both sure of it.

If the first time didn't create Junior, this time certainly did. Yes, the love between a man and a woman was a beautiful thing, when it was done the way their Heavenly Father intended it. Their marriage meant he was all hers, and she was his alone. They were both sure of something else. They were sure they were soul mates. It had taken them a while to discover that obvious fact, but now they knew it, for only soul mates had the power to touch each other's souls.

They had an important day tomorrow, and Atylk was certainly glad she would have her husband by her side. That thought, *my husband*, was all she needed to lull her to sleep. She whispered a prayer of thanks to the Lord before sleep took her over.

Epilogue

It was Easter that weekend and everyone was at Sunday service. The sermon wasn't what Atylk would typically hear on Easter Sunday. The pastor spoke from the scripture about what would happen in the last days. He also pointed out that there were some things that we couldn't and shouldn't ascribe to luck. Luck wasn't a guarantee to eternal life.

As with everything, Atylk always tried to apply life's lessons, and so as she looked around the church and saw Pam and Jason, it seemed prophetic that she would get what she wanted. They had finally conceived after they stopped taking the medication the doctor prescribed. When he spoke about those who hunt for luck, she glanced over at Shirley and Trevor, who took a chance at each other. They believed in their dreams and had produced a beautiful family. Trevor had what Atylk's grandmother would call a "live spirit," and so he dreamt a lot. He would always share his dreams with Shirley.

Atylk remembered one dream in particular that Shirley shared with her at their sleepover. It was about a white sheep, a black ram goat, and lambs of many different colors. Wolves were homing in on them. The white sheep kept circling the colored lambs trying to protect them. The sheep soon got dizzy and fell down. The lambs bleated to the ram goat for help, but he just ran off. The colored lambs scattered about, and just as the sheep tried to get up on her feet in a panic, she saw the black goat in the distance. What looked like a big guard dog was on the right, and there was a smaller but equally fierce one on the left, and a behind them were the colored lambs. All were encompassed in a transparent dome-shaped structure, which was moving quickly towards the sheep. The halo, a force field of some kind, covered the sheep just in time as the vicious attacks from the wolves just bounced off the bubble.

At the time she thought Shirley was babbling from her hangover, but as Atylk looked at them now she could see how her grandmother would interpret that dream. *What a wonderful thing it is to be in a family the way it was intended*, Atylk thought. You have to be a real selfless individual to invite another person to share your space and time. She had learned that one of the greatest joys in life was to see another person smile and know that you're responsible for putting that smile there. That's what families do for each other, despite the many things threatening to tear them apart. For that reason alone the family should be protected at all cost.

David, Trevor's younger brother, had journeyed away from his spiritual upbringing when his mom divorced his dad. His world was simply shattered. David thought Trevor was foolish when he got married, but deep down he wanted the same thing his brother had.

He had dated every woman that came his way. He wasn't a player, he was sure to tell them he was not the marrying type. They came at their own risk. His male friends admired his skills with the ladies, but he knew that he had broken a few hearts, even though he didn't mean to.

As he got older his priorities changed. He realized he needed to forgive his mother. Her betrayal of his father was controlling him, so much so that the more women he had the more uneasy he felt. He should have been happy, but he wasn't. Too many birthdays to remember, too many presents to buy, and too many dates to go on. At times he went to the movies three times in one week to see the *same* movie. Funny thing, his brother and his dad didn't seem to mind that his mom had walked out on them. All his dad said when he asked how he could be so calm was that "life happens." In life, he explained, when you fall you have to get up and press on. He didn't get it, though, until he turned his life around. When Judith's son Jeff came to him for advice about women, because he wanted to be like him, he realized what a bad example he was setting. That's when he decided to get in touch with his spirit man, instead of being lead by his flesh. The younger boys in his community thought what he was doing was admirable and there was nothing to admire about taking women's emotions lightly.

As he became a mentor for Jeff and showed him he didn't need to feel pressured to smoke and do what his friends did to feel like a man, it dawned on him that he needed to lead by example. As his spiritual journey began, he realized that there was only one woman who would not accept his confirmed bachelor lifestyle if he wanted to be with her. There was only one woman who he constantly thought of no matter where he was or who he was with. And there was only one woman who would stand up to him and tell him what a jerk he was when he was being one. So David married her.

Then there were people like Atylk and Judith, who had no one to defend them, no one they could count on, yet they had a vision for themselves and would not rest until they had attained it. They refused to use their past as an excuse to fail. Were they simply just lucky, or were they just reaping the benefits of their hard work?

David sat on Atylk's right and her daughter Salo sat on her left. No, luck certainly didn't have anything to do with the way things turned out for her at least. It was simply the right attitude and hard work. You see they all needed to realize where their strength came from first and foremost. There were simply some things that were beyond them. Some things required divine intervention, some things required help from above. With that in place they then needed to realize their motivation. Why they needed to press on, and it was always about their children and their family.

You see, it wasn't Slygo who took Judith's "stuff." It was her very own son who did it. It crushed Judith so badly, because she knew firsthand how important it was to protect helpless children. She was once in that vulnerable spot. To think that she could bring harm to her own child was too much for her to take. This *little* drug problem she had was one of those pebbles in her path. She didn't see it, but when she stumbled she knew it was time to turn things around.

Like Atylk, she too had grown up in church. But they all went only because they were told to. They did it because everyone around them did it. They all belonged to different religious denominations, and it was only when they got older that they realized it wasn't about religion but rather their relationship with God. Until they understood that pivotal fact, it didn't matter how much money they made—they needed more. Neither did it matter what things they bought to make them happy—they had no joy. And it didn't matter who lay next to them for comfort—they had no peace. Nor could they understand the significance or precious value of love from above—for they needed to show it to each other first.

Judith got help for both herself and her son. The hardest part for her was admitting she needed help in the first place. But sure enough, once she did, things came together much easier for her. Within a year she launched her own clothing line. She already had the notoriety. Good or bad everyone knew her name, so it made her line marketable and it did quite well, putting her up there with all the other top local designers. They all worked hard to get where they had gotten. No mistaking that. Judith and John married and she realized how blessed she was to have a man like him in her life. She realized she not only needed professional help, but more importantly, she needed God's help. It was only a week after she *thought* John had rejected her, that she called him over to talk. She talked, he listened, and when he was done listening, he was prepared to commit to protecting and sheltering her with a ring of engagement. He loved her, with all her flaws, and for that reason alone she wanted to be the best wife she could possibly be. So she turned her life over to God after that day, and she hasn't been the same since.

It was a moment of reflection for them all. They all thought back to their childhood as the sermon went on. Jason remembered his dad bringing home gifts for both him and his mother. It made them both happy, because there was no reason for it. It wasn't anyone's birthday or anything; he just bought things because he could afford to. His father worked long hard hours to make them happy. He vowed to make as much, if not more, than his dad did. But it was only now, as a grown man, that he realized his father was always too tired to play with him. He didn't think it affected his childhood, because his mother was always cheerful and happy and would play with him. When he got old enough he simply went off and played with the boys in the village. He didn't think his mom would have been as happy if she couldn't do all that shopping though.

But he now knew he was scared to death of being a father, because he had no idea how to be one. Sure he could provide. He certainly could discipline. That much he had learned from his dad, but he had no idea how to interact, how to show affection to his own son. He didn't let that thought overwhelm him, though; he was ready to learn. He had straightened things up with his finances, even though it meant starting over. It was tough, real tough, because his dad had died two years before this all happened and had left him a tiny fortune. Yet in no time it seemed he couldn't even find a quarter to put in the parking meter. Words couldn't explain how happy he was that Pam stood by him. He loved her a lot before, but even more so now, because he knew what it took for her to look past his physical appearance and see the man on the inside. Sure he had taken the easy way out and opted for surgery to lose the weight, but he still had a long way to go.

As Pam sat next to him, she too remembered the first time she read the words "Obsessive Compulsive Disorder." She knew something was off at her house; she just couldn't name it. She was thirteen years old when she went to her school's library and looked it up. The words jumped off the computer screen, like someone pointing an accusing finger at her. She jumped back in her seat then looked behind her to ensure no one else had seen what she was looking at. She had gotten a beating from her mom that morning. She had seen her mom get smacked around by her dad before, but it was the first time for her. She had always known what needed to be done at her house; she had just forgotten that night. She was all taken up with these new feelings she had for Jason, and she hadn't remembered to close the kitchen shades. The sun glared through the kitchen window at a time in the morning when her dad needed to read his morning paper. It annoyed him so much that it became one of her many daily chores. They had to be closed when he came out for breakfast.

Her friends thought her parents were weird, and for that reason no one came to her house. It didn't seem strange to her though. What she strongly disapproved of was the way Atylk sometimes left her bed unmade. Or the chaos that went on at Shirley's house. What was odd to her was the way Judith's mom only had their lawn cut twice a month and not every week like she did. No one's house was really untidy, but there was a marked difference in hers. Her house was like a mini-museum. Everything was dusted, shined, polished, and in place at her house. No shoes from outside were allowed on the carpet. All the forks and knives had to be turned down when she did dishes. The grapes had to be washed, dried with paper towel, and picked off the vine before going into the fridge. Their grocery bags didn't come in the house; they were unloaded at the door by her and wiped down with paper towel and natural cleaning agents by her mom. There were no hand towels in her bathrooms. They were always stocked with paper towel.

You could eat off their kitchen floor—that's how clean it was. It all made Pam behave in a way that made her friends not like her very much and she didn't understand why. Her parents weren't doing anything wrong. As a matter of fact, for each assignment she was given there was a logical reason why it needed to be done. But Lord it wore her down sometimes. It made her over-think the simplest things.

Trevor just looked at his family and was thankful that what he didn't get genetically he made up for practically. No one in his family went to college. Not his mom or dad or brother. They were simply hard working people who applied muscle to get by. They owned the local farm and that's how they acquired their wealth. Not that they were rich by any means, but they did okay. Their dad was looked up to and well respected in the community. He did all right in school, but he knew he wasn't cut out to be a doctor or anything of that nature. He knew he was good with his hands, and he was blessed to have a woman in his life to help him use that gift. She was no fool, mind you—he couldn't quit his day job until his business was bringing in steady money—but she stood by him and his dream all the way.

He reached over and touched her hand for good measure.

Shirley hardly noticed. She was too busy keeping the boys in check, while her heart ached because her daughters were not present. They had both gotten old enough to move out of her house and although she was proud of them she couldn't help but wonder if she had pushed them away sooner than they needed to go. She just didn't like chaos. It was that way in her house when she was growing up and she just wanted things organized. Why couldn't they see that? Trevor kept assuring her that they would come around, but she wished they were still at home. She missed cooking for a large family, and if they were living at home, surely they would be in church.

They all focused their attention back to the pulpit as the pastor concluded his sermon. There was so much truth in what the preacher was saying. They would have no one to blame but themselves if they missed out on heaven. They all had excuses why they behaved the way they did. They could blame a number of people who did them wrong. But this was about them personally; this wasn't a time for them to count on luck to get there. They all had to give an account of what they did with this awesome life and body they were blessed with. They were responsible for their own actions. They all needed to release the fear of failing, of not getting there, and embrace the joy and peace that would come from doing what was right. They all knew for sure what the question was: could they do it? Could they do it before they had no time left in which to do it? Only time would tell. Yep, time was the key element in their lives. This day they had been blessed with. This hour of worship, this minute to say "Thank you" or "I love you" or "I miss you and I need you," what would they do with it and who would they say it to? Some said it to the person across from them before church came to a close. But who would say it, mean it, and look towards heaven while doing it was a mystery. The only ones who knew the answer were the individuals themselves.

But Atylk continually prayed that her friends would see the truth of God's tender mercies and loving kindness, the way she had. The truth was they couldn't lift their hands from their sides to their chests without His approval. No amount of fame or money could prevent a stroke that could render them immobile. Every venture they undertook was only made possible because God allowed it, yet they so often failed to thank Him. Their financial security couldn't prevent death if it came knocking. But all Atylk could do was pray for their salvation. She too was once walking through life in darkness, although it all seemed clear to her now.

The following day Atylk sat in her conference room and thought about her grandmother. She always said you can't hold fire and water in the same hand. Later in life Atylk read that you couldn't serve two masters. She was done taking advice from her friends. She prayed about things instead, and in so doing let go of her fears and gave herself up to be used as an instrument of God, knowing he would only bring good character-building things her way. She now knew that this moment was meant to be because of all that she had been through.

Remembering her near drowning incident as a child was perhaps something she shouldn't be thinking about right now but she couldn't help it. Only now did she realize that every bad situation had to come to an end. And although at the time she could see the shore she was determined to reach, there were times in her life when she *couldn't* see the shore, or any sign of light at the end of the tunnel. But God could. He knew she would be okay. If only she had mastered the art of trusting Him sooner, her life might have been that much less difficult. By no means was she a victim. Every bad situation she found herself in was her own doing. But to be honest she was thankful for her life's journey. It made her the woman she was today.

Today her perfectly toned chocolate skin glowed in the light of the conference room. There were no bruises, and no scars anywhere on her body. Her skin was flawless, actually. Yet a few years ago she was possibly the most damaged woman you could meet. Her scars were buried so deep beneath her skin that it would have taken a miracle worker to heal them. The pain inflicted by those scars was the worst kind. The pain from a cut stops hurting eventually, but these emotional cuts, these bruises were the kind you couldn't see with your eyes. These cuts were the most painful to bear and hardest to treat. They didn't show when they would hurt by bleeding. Neither could they be measured or diagnosed by the pints of blood lost. This pain showed up when she least expected or wanted it, and it wouldn't leave until *it* was ready to go. This pain threatened to control her very destiny, by messing with one of her most of vital organs: *her mind*.

This pain made Atylk and her friends do foolish things they would later regret. Go to places they shouldn't be. Partake in conversations that tear down rather than build up and then say things they couldn't take back. It made them watch things they had no business looking at and, worse yet, consume things that destroyed their body, only to have them pray for a miracle after to heal it. Yes this pain was a silent killer all right. It is such a tricky and clever pain that no human could cure it. Why? Because it brings on not only a physical death but a spiritual one as well. Yes, this pain needed a special miracle worker, and his name was Jesus.

Today was a new day, a new era for Atylk. The same way person looked at a scar on their hand and remembered an incident in their past, good or bad. That was the same way she looked at her emotional scars. No longer did she hide them. They were as much a part of her as she was a part of them. Her emotional scars showed up when she cried at a dumb play, or when she danced to the song that talked about every pimple being exactly where it's supposed to be. She knew who she was now and needed no one to affirm her. She had no father, yet she was the daughter of a King. She was complex all right, but her true friends loved and understood her, and to those who didn't she would forever be an enigma. She gave her love to a source that wouldn't manipulate it or take advantage of it. For the most part, they didn't know how. She gave her love to her husband and the children, and it filled her with a joy that she couldn't even attempt to explain to anyone, and she didn't need to either. Yes, she was finally at a place where she could experience joy at work *and* at home. It was a good feeling to have a man in her life who she could say she knew loved her dearly.

She glanced over at him, and a sweet smile spread across her face.

Yes, Atylk had come a long way. She had learned and continued to learn a lot about life and love. But if there was only one lesson she could leave with her daughter, it would be to live life to its fullest, laugh like there's no tomorrow, grow to her tallest heights, and love as if she had never been hurt—do it the way little children do. But she should do it all through her Heavenly Father's eyes. For no matter how old they got in life, they were always going to be someone's child. They were all just little children inside, and they got hurt just as easily. They had simply mastered the art of masking it as they got older. It was a simple question of whose son or daughter they wanted to be. Someone famous? Someone wealthy? Someone evil? Or someone omnipresent, omnipotent, and omniscient?

It's a choice. It's always been that way, He never changes.

Ironic the way life sometimes turns out. Her spokesman was once a little boy labeled as "slow." His name was Danny and for more reasons than one she couldn't be more proud of him. As she saw pictures of the children's faces for their ID cards being plastered against the wall, Atylk again had to bring herself back to the task at hand. Life was filled with imperfections and she was one of them. So she had too many things, too many ideas going on in her head.

That's one of the reasons she hired a spokesman. He could deliver and promote the policies and campaigns they had worked so long and hard to establish.

The spokesman began,

"Our boys and girls club's motto is 'Break the Cycle.' You may ask, "What cycle needs to be broken?". But the mere fact that we have to ask is in itself a problem. You see, we are faced with an epidemic of grave proportions. It is so serious that no medication can cure it. Ladies and gentlemen, we are failing our children and we continue to fail them with each generation. That cycle of failure continues if we do nothing.

"Children are just that—children—and they live what they've learned. What exactly have we taught them? We allow our boys to run wild yet hold on to our girls and teach them the importance of being beautiful, knowing how to cook and clean, so that someday those same wild boys will be tame enough to take care of a family.

"Yes, making a family is something our girls have learned very well. The only problem is that we have way too many single-parent families. It's all around us. Our men are missing in action. But how can we blame them? Our men are simply exhibiting learned behavior.

Atylk was looking around the room as he spoke and she could see that some were not at all happy about what was being said. Some were mumbling under their breath, others sat up erect in their chairs, arms folded across their chest. However, by the time he pressed a button in his hand and the screen lit up with bar graphs and pie charts to support his argument there was a noticeable change in their demeanor. He showed the statistics and the reputable organization that compiled the data and suddenly there was now a more solemn and sincere look of concern among some of them.

"God in his divine wisdom created man first, to lead, to take charge. He *then* created a woman to be his *help* mate. The tables are turned when our women have to cry out for help from our men with their children. God asked man to claim dominion over the animals, not to behave like them. The goats and pigs around us have no obligation other than to eat, mate, and multiply. That's the extent of their mental capacity.

"Let's take a look back at what's been happening to us over the years. Our women are taught to take care of themselves and their homes in hopes that our men will do the right thing. Our women shouldn't hope; they need to insist that our men do what's right. Are we really saying to our children that the extent of our mental capacity is to become a society of fatherless people struggling to get by? At what point will we teach our women to hold on to their virtue, for it is more valuable than gold, more precious than rubies. When it comes to our children there is no room for hope. Rather, there is an urgency to protect, teach, and provide.

He spoke with such eloquence and passion that Atylk could see he was getting through to them.

"Something is wrong when the law has to *insist* a man take care of his offspring. Something is wrong when our women think they have to prove their love and loyalty to our men by bearing children *first*. The quest to look good for our men suggests to some of our women that it's alright to rack up debt far beyond what is acceptable. The quest to have money in their pockets at all cost turns some of our men into lawless thugs. Something is **seriously** wrong when our young men look to prisoners for an acceptable dress code, then make a point of it to carry themselves like old men. Pants falling off, shirts three times their size. At what point did our women learn that the *less* they wear they are *more* beautiful they are? How did our children learn this? When did they learn that this is acceptable? They learned it when we said nothing, when we remained silent and did nothing. Quite frankly silence **is** a spoken language.

At this point some men were touching their chins or faces as if in deep thought. Whenever the spokesman paused there was dead silence in the room.

"Today our boys and girls club's theme is 'I am a leader, not a follower." We intend to be like a rock falling into a pond and have a ripple effect on our society by saying, 'Break the Cycle.' By having our girls say to their brothers, 'I need your help inside with the dishes.' By asking those men who *are* fathers in their homes to talk to our young men about preparing for *a* family while young by saving, investing, and becoming entrepreneurs before it is too late and they have to provide for four families, yet being there for none. Something is wrong, ladies and gentlemen, when we are all followers. Someone has to lead. We come with a message to our men to lead. Lead on and walk in their God-given destiny by honoring and valuing our women for their true worth. Our club will send forth the message that our women need to first see and appreciate their worth, for they are the ones with the power to create life. They have the power to demand the best from our men. They have the power to turn lost boys into strong, powerful men when they insist that they become that—strong men, mighty men, men of valor.

"**That** is our main purpose here. However, for those dealing with the profitable aspect of this venture, bear this in mind: Yes, we have to make a profit to be able to have prolonged success, but let's not miss how this all intertwines. Clearly, we have the potential among our youth to inspire them to think and come to us with their ideas if they need help implementing those ideas. This country has a **ninety-eight** percent literacy rate. It is quite obvious that intellect is not the problem. Instilling moral value is as of equal importance, if not more, if we hope to have a balanced society.

He paused for a minute, and Atylk wasn't quite sure if it was to let that thought register or if it was because of the emotion she saw in his eyes. Perhaps it was a bit of both. She knew he was as equally committed to this mission as she was.

"For those who may ask, 'Why should I care?' Or 'How does this affect me?' Let's think about it for a minute. If there are only a handful of major companies around ready to hire the thousands of young people graduating this year—and the year after, and the year after that—how long will it be before there is no employment left? What will happen to our society if no one is inspired to start their own business? Dare I say that the sheer need to survive will only result in a life of crime for our youth? We have to be proactive instead of waiting until our cars are stolen or our homes are invaded to then react. It affects us when our taxpayer dollars have to be spent on people on welfare who, because they are irresponsible or simply ignorant, would rather buy a phone or new sneakers instead of food for their children. Or worse yet, when those dollars have to be spent building more prisons instead of schools or libraries.

Some heads were now shaking as if the truth was finally registering.

"We are very much aware that we can't save everyone. Quite frankly, some won't want to be saved. There will always be those who are satisfied with living from paycheck to paycheck. However, for those who aspire to have more, to reach higher heights, there must be a place where they can go to make that possible. It's not an easy way out we are providing; for many, it's sheer determination that will decide their ultimate success. But for those who want that success, there must be a place where people who have had all the wrong odds in life thrown at them can come to for rescue, where they can turn their trials into triumphs. Let's face it, we aren't all scholars, so if all they come with is their two hands and the will to make a better life, we should be honored that we are in a position to offer the help they need with their own hands in our Tradespersons Program.

By this point Atylk had no doubt that they realized that The Unit meant business.

"Throughout this meeting, our PRO, Mr. Wilkinson, will enlighten you on the other programs being offered. For now, I want to talk about…"

As she listened to him, she was sure she had made the right choice. As her grandmother would say…

For goodness' sake, Atylk, palease stop with the "Grandmother would say" business, she scolded herself. She had to cover her mouth to stifle her giggle. *So unladylike and unprofessional* she thought. Living would be in vain if she couldn't laugh, but now certainly wasn't the time for it.

Yes, life is good. It's meant to be enjoyed to the fullest, but in the right way. In His way, in His will.

Breinigsville, PA USA
26 July 2010
242420BV00001B/4/P